'If you haven't read Jen Calleja's novel yet, then you definitely should... it's politically insightful, funny, formally inventive and addictive reading!'
    – **Rosanna Mclaughlin**

'I'm reading *Vehicle* for the s into my dreams. What a glo
    – **Katy Derbyshire**

Praise for *Goblinhood: Goblin as a Mode*

'Follow Jen Calleja down whatever path she leads you: she is a sage and enchanting guide.'
    – **Kate Simpson, *The Telegraph***

'It's just as bonkers and brilliant as it sounds.'
    – **Barry Pierce, *HERO Magazine***

'Something akin to Philip Roth's *Portnoy's Complaint* or Katharina Volckmer's *The Appointment*: a virtuoso exercise in free-association'
    – **Oscar Mardell, 3:*AM Magazine***

'I urge readers to join Jen Calleja in hot pursuit of the goblin through contemporary culture in this unexpected, revelatory, and frequently totally hilarious book, which is also at turns politically urgent and moving, as Calleja weaves the sorrows and joys of her own life into this critical and kaleidoscopic text.'
    – **Rebecca May Johnson**

'Jen Calleja takes a throwaway internet trend and turns it inside out in a series of glorious, out-there essays. Demented and luxurious in equal parts.'
    – **Anna Bogutskaya**

Jen Calleja

Fair

( )   (   )

Praise for *Vehicle*

'*Vehicle* manages to reproduce the near-physical thrill of archive discovery while also being a playful, resistant and gorgeously compelling game with text and language. Calleja is one of the most exciting writers working today.'
    – **Kaliane Bradley**

'*Vehicle* is unlike anything I have read before, a brilliantly original piece of work, it blew my mind. Reading it was like hearing The Velvet Underground for the first time!'
    – **Camilla Grudova**

'To say that *Vehicle* is a feminist *Pale Fire* for the Brexit generation may not be high enough praise for this intoxicating, thrilling and endlessly inventive work.'
    – **Joanna Walsh**

'A high-stakes speculation, an adventure into a new world order as well as the possibilities of the novel-form, *Vehicle* is a feat of ungovernable imagination. Bold, bracing, brilliant.'
    – **Kate Briggs**

'Jen Calleja's debut novel towers with ambition that proves justified through *Vehicle*'s meticulous world-building, pin-sharp characterisation and mordant wit.'
    – **Buzz Magazine**

'With its dashes of, oh, I don't know, Quin, Pynchon, Chute, Gibson and Ballard, Jen Calleja's mind-blowing mix of secret-state hatred of the other, alt culture and written word-power has produced a compulsive future classic. I loved *Vehicle*. Totally recommended.'
    – **The Crack Magazine**

The Life-Art of Translation

'Dante himself puts forward the standard medieval justification that an author can talk about himself if he thinks what he has to say will benefit his readers or if he has to defend his reputation.'
   – **Peter Hainsworth, 'New Life: Tracing the beauty and inconsistency in the work of Dante'**

'I feel at home in hall 6, I feel confident there. All the other halls are funhouses of lights and headshots and I even once found myself in the business hall where I was cut badly by a crisp Windsor knot.'
   – **CJ Evans, X**

'The translator has no being, should neither be seen nor heard, should be (yawn) faithful, should be (double yawn) a plate of glass. Well, *Kerrang!!!*'
   – **Michael Hofmann, 'Sharp Biscuit – Some Thoughts on Translating'**

Contents

Welcome – Glossary of Terms / Terms and Conditions

I've been working on something spectacular.

Have you ever been to a book fair? An art fair? How about a fun fair? Those vast constellations in exhibition centres the size of aircraft carriers, or akin to airports with their own escalators and travelators, or in custom-made tents the size of a giant's wedding marquee, or a garish sprawl of gaudy attractions and hazardous-looking rides. Wildly different to zine fairs in community halls or in the backrooms of pubs, the print fairs in cafés and shop basements, or the little cartoon vehicles for kids in supermarkets that gently rock you back and forth.

Art fairs and book fairs dissect cavernous floor space into room-sized (how big is a room?) cubicles where you, the visitor, suspend your disbelief. You're not in a huge hall with voices ricocheting around and raining down on you like you're in an underground cave: you're in a calm gallery, you're in a private office, shouting with your face but whispering.

A cubicle or stand might be a simple white box with three walls and a patch of carpet or faux wooden floor, a few paintings or sculptures on plinths, a desk and chairs and some shelves displaying books. It might have a technicolour pond dotted with glitter sunken mysteriously into the floor, or a giant inflatable Felix the Cat. The big galleries like to show off and create immersive spaces like a perfect recreation of an artist's studio or an interactive game like an uncanny fairground experience. Big-name houses take up twice, thrice, four times, eight times the floorplan of other presses, with columns, huge billboards, the dazzle and potential of a rollercoaster.

Sudden happenings like dances, provocations, roving parades and people in costume occur in the spaces between or in front of the stands, appearing and disappearing as if in a dream.

The whole thing is one big performance. These places aren't serious, spacious pantheons of trade; they're circus tops. Fairground, fairy tale, mirage. It's like when the fair rolls into town. I think of these fairs like pop-up theatres. Pop-up shops.

When I was interviewed to work on the information desk at a big, week-long art fair pitched up in a vast park the summer after graduating from my postgrad degree, I was asked by the interviewer to describe what an art fair is. I said that it was kind of, like, a big supermarket? There are aisles upon aisles of stands where gallerists display their goods. Only without the trolleys!

The interviewer didn't like this answer. I didn't get the job. But then I did get the job. In the end, they didn't have enough people to turn anyone down.

It was a tiring job where I had to deal with a lot of rude, entitled people who wouldn't look at me as they asked where the VIP lounge was, and would walk off *tout de suite* once they had their answer to quaff the champagne laid on by the sponsor. The next year, my friend, who managed the guided tours, asked if I would like to curate and lead tours around the art fair instead.

I did this for three consecutive summers. I walked around the not-yet-fair a couple of days before the grand opening, picking pieces I found the most interesting, researching them, then planned my route. The fair would still be in an unfinished state, planks of wood and offcuts of tape littering the aisles, and last-minute changes would occur. I would come in early each day to make sure one of the pieces on my tour hadn't been sold or swapped overnight – an eerie feeling to walk up to one of the stands and find everything as it was, yet one of the pieces transformed into something else or a doorway moved to a different side of a stand, like an enchanted labyrinth.

The tours would last an hour and I would perform them – they really were a performance – three to six times a day. I would wear a head mic, and as I led them around the packed fair the tour groups would listen to me speaking on headphones plugged into transmitters on lanyards set to my frequency. Sometimes they would listen avidly and ask questions, others would half-listen, some would chat the whole time, a few would wander off or hand me back the equipment while I was mid-flow because they had spotted someone they knew, or the tour wasn't what they had expected. Maybe you will do the same.

I would sometimes lie down under the information desk between tours and close my eyes; it was exhausting. The bigger publishers at book fairs have doors on their stands that lead into private broom-cupboard offices. I've power-napped in one of those too. It's like being underwater. A hot, noiseless, airless pocket in a ship's hull, a cruise liner of interactions, activities and entertainment.

I can remember how disorientating a big fair can be. The noise, the lack of air, how overcrowded it is, the feeling that you're getting ill, 'fair flu' on the horizon. The way that the stands and cubicles appear open to all but are actually strangely closed. For most of them you need an appointment, and yet you're not sure how to get one.

Stick with me, I'll look after you.

At book fairs, I would have a rendezvous or an author reading I'd like to watch on one side of the fair, and then have a matter of minutes to rush to the other side for a casual chat with an old friend who might have a lead on a translation job. I'd go up escalators and take lifts, go down stairwells I'd suddenly realise weren't open to the public, overshoot an aisle. I'd fly by panel discussions and sporadic parties I could look in on but couldn't be part of, and rush past rows of one-on-one meetings that looked like the first round of a major chess tournament. I'd rubberneck people having free shoulder massages in the middle of the main corridor through the fair and spot some others lolling on beanbags in a dark corner by a fire exit. Everyone always late and apologising for being late.

No one will ever be late at my fair, everyone will be right on time.

I've been building this fair, my own fair, out at sea, just off the coast of Hastings. You can take a ferry or use the bridge. The main structure was built with the same treated timber as Hastings Pier, and clad in the dark, iridescent, hand-glazed ceramic tiles used on Hastings Contemporary art gallery, which were originally selected to match the deep black of the higgledy-piggledy fishermen's huts on the seafront. We had to be in keeping with the vernacular of the town to get planning permission.

I forget how we got the funding in the first place; you probably wouldn't be interested in that anyway.

There's something lopsided about my fair, too, but it's by design. We've secured partnerships with local bookshops and galleries, as well as the various amusements, including Funland and Playland and, of course, the Hastings pleasure pier itself.

It's a Translation Fair, a Translator Fair. A fair themed around the life and work of a single literary translator. Just as Christine de Pizan wrote *The Book of the City of Ladies* (translated by <u>Rosalind Brown-Grant</u>; get used to me underlining the importance of translators) to build a fictional city to write good things about women, this is a fair built to write good (and bad, and OK) things about translators, about a translator.

It's an art/book/fun fair, but also a medieval walled city, a mall, a multiplex, a multimedia arts centre. It's multipurpose. An epic maze of stands, stalls, booths, installations, rides, arcades, a canteen, a cinema, spread almost infinitely across a single, spacious level that hovers over the water on stilts and looks no larger than a bungalow.

When we open tomorrow – to great fanfare! free entry! accessible! – visitors will be able to explore the fair on their own or with friends, or join an audio tour, wearing headsets so my voice can steer and commentate directly into their heads.

You have been selected for this prototype tour, wandering with me around the echoey, half-finished space while I draft and rehearse my spiel as the painting gets finished, the walls are put up, the carpet is rolled out and trimmed, the stages are built, the artwork is mounted, the speakers are installed, the games are tested, the cats are fed.

Where once tour attendees and those I was about to meet to talk books would spot me sneakily retying my Doc Martens, straightening my navy corduroy pinafore dress, scraping my hair into a high bun and pinning up the short bits at the nape of my neck, badly reapplying lipstick on lips chapped from the air-conditioning, quickly downing an espresso – my routine before every tour I gave as a seasonal guide and between every other meeting with editors and agents – you'll now get a peek of me around the corner of a ride retying my Vans, scrunching and poofing my mullet, unwedgying a denim jumpsuit, creasing my face to will my glasses back up my nose, or will it be tightening my Salomon hiking trainers, reticking my eyeliner and de-linting a black Adidas tracksuit?

Just before I begin, let me check I have my name badge pinned on. It reads:

JEN CALLEJA (ca – lay – yer)

The same name you can see in purple neon on the side of the fair at night, its reflection distorted on the black tiles and the even blacker water. I'm making an exhibition of myself, making a lucky dip of my life.

Threshold / Balloon Arch

Someone once told me that they weren't really interested in reading about the life of a literary translator and far more so in the art of translation, presuming that these two things can be separated, maybe thinking that the art of translation is something neutral and untouched and singular. If you're not interested in the life part, you can skip to the end, do not pass go, do not collect... I should just offer up my experiences extracted from their contexts, perhaps. But where's the fun in that? I think that, much like a word or phrase removed from the neutrality of the dictionary and placed unthinkingly into a sentence, it would lack meaning; I think, in fact, that it would be meaningless.

To enter the Fair, you go through this magnificent balloon arch. Each mirror-silver balloon has the words 'the art of translation' or 'the craft of translation' or 'the act of translation' written on it in thick, black, Shrigleyesque scrawl; you can pull or tug or wrench them off the scaffold as you enter, anchor them to you by their long black ribbons.

A1 – Where the Magic Happens

The first thing you see once through the plucked arch is a recreation of my desk set-up just as it is right now, today. My desk is in a room in my house, next to my partner's desk. Pinned up around it is a slip of paper I found in a library copy of translator Willa Muir's dual-memoir *Belonging*, that says, 'Willa at one with the universe, p.31'; a photo of my new nephew so I remember that he's out there and I am in a way responsible for him; a local French tutor's business card showing a picture of Kermit the Frog in French garb asking in a speech bubble, 'Parlez-vous français?'

The desk is in a corner in front of a window that looks down into a yard at the back of my house. If you look through this wooden window frame, painted white to look like plastic, you'll see some rubber replica ivy hanging directly outside the plexiglass, though in reality the real ivy is further away. You get the idea though. On the windowsill is a metal Yves Klein-blue or bright navy book cradle holding the books I'm currently translating. I should really be working on these projects, this whole fair is one big bout of procrastination. *Do the job!* can be my mantra when I'm hesitating to begin in the morning.

I currently have three books on the go, at different stages of completion:

an experimental long-form memoir-essay by a German author based in Berlin is going through final edits;
a surreal novel by a Swiss author based in Basel is nearly finished;
and a darkly comic, interlinked short story collection by a Serbian author based in Vienna is about to be started.

I've daydreamed of putting pictures of every author I've ever translated up on my wall. Here are quartets of passport photos of these three authors, I'm going to pin them on my wall next to my desk right now, like I'm a fan, like they're religious icons, like they're my friends or extended family, like they're beloved and feared leaders, like they're my crush.

The author often doesn't get a say in who translates their work, we're often thrown together into this working relationship by publishers. Maybe I should pin up the logos of publishers, too? They are the ones who commission me, the ones to have luckily selected me from dozens of translators. Translating literary works from German into English is my job, I'm paid to do it, and over the last thirteen years I've translated around twenty books, each translation taking anywhere from four to twelve months, depending on complexity, depending on what else I have on. Half my time is spent translating books, the other half writing my own books, with some short-term teaching and long-term residencies among all this, but translation is where I make most of my income. In almost every case, I have been commissioned by a publisher in London or a regional UK town, or North America or Australia, to translate a book so that they can publish it in English. They come to me because this is what I do, it's what I'm known for.

Most days I sit with the book I'm working on laid open on a stand, and depending on what draft I'm on, I'm either:

reading and automatically writing down the first translation of a line that comes to mind, or multiple versions of the same line separated by slashes, or [...] when I don't know or have forgotten the word or phrase – no peeking at the dictionary or the Internet;

double-checking my translation against the original to make sure I haven't missed anything or to see if I have a new solution on this new day;

or I might be checking words or lines that have eluded or bothered me right from the start, staring at them, hoping they might let me put them to bed now we're reaching the end, trimming down my questions for the author.

I sometimes take these books for a walk to a café or a train ride in order to remember what it's like to simply read them in the world, to fantasise that I am just a reader taking it in in that relaxed, readerly way, but sometimes I relish leaving their burden at home, escaping them, locking them in.

I'm often commissioned to read books in German and write reports on them for publishers. They've heard on the grapevine that a novel is good, but they can't read it in-house, so they ask me to read it and tell them everything about it: what it's about, the writing style, whether it would translate well, and, crucially, whether I think it's good enough. I'll read the book, mull it over, write my report – not for much money, there's the same problem for those who read play scripts, intense reading and decisiveness for not much compensation – usually all within a week or two, all while translating.

Sometimes I'll be translating shorter pieces, a poem or a dozen poems, a short story, for magazines – they might have asked me, or I've submitted to them.

I might get commissioned by a publisher in Frankfurt or Hamburg to translate an excerpt from a novel so they can use it to pitch the translation rights to English-language publishers.

Now and again, an author might get in touch, asking if they can commission me directly.

Pass around these forty sets of passport photos and pin them up on the wall around the desk, authors I've met fleetingly via their work. I do these 'smaller' projects in the gaps between book-length projects, or to overlap with my already overlapping bigger projects, when I don't really have the time but feel my energy is flagging and I can't resist a cheeky boost from something else, a palate cleanser, but also, the money.

When I translate a book I get paid half up front and half on sub-mission, instant gratification for delayed pay, which means the money runs out before I'm finished, it's a recurring loop, hence why

I accept the next book when it's offered in the middle of another project, hence that 'quick' extra project.

The days can be long, my weekends curtailed. I spend my time not staring at photos of the author, out there in the world somewhere, in Germany, Austria, Switzerland, on a residency in Russia or America or Rome, but gazing into a page in the privacy of this little room.

You'll find me sitting here, though of course you won't, because it's my house, and no one sees me working. There are times when I look up from my computer and think with a smile, an eye roll, a furrowed brow: what the hell am I doing? How did I end up here?

If everyone's tried out the desk chair and looked at the photos, we can really get started.

Broom Cupboard

Over there you'll see an inconspicuous wooden door dented at the bottom where someone's tried to kick it in, revealing it's just a cheap hollow frame of no substance.

Sorry, it's a bit of a squeeze.

Twenty years ago, I submitted a form where I'd painstakingly placed an 'X' in boxes next to the subjects I wanted to take at A-level: Art, French, English Literature, German.

English was my subject, it was the one thing I was good at. But I found learning languages perplexing and challenging, I couldn't stop thinking about them. In my GCSEs I'd got a B in French and an A in German, and this latter grade once landed me at a one-off Saturday school session for promising German-learners, where I spent the whole day saying nothing after realising I really didn't know any German. I stood numb with fear, watching as students from other local, mostly private, schools were practically fluent. I was no linguistic Wunderkind.

The language lessons at school were quite chaotic, the prospect of learning languages made pupils hysterical. The teachers were essentially having to do crowd control the whole time, and if they tried to speak to us only in French or German, there would be wailing and laughter. We were told repeatedly that it wasn't our fault; languages were just very difficult. This made me even more intrigued.

During German, I sat in the back right-hand corner with my boyfriend, where we spent most of the time whispering to each other, rocking on the wobbly chairs, hands under the desks. French felt more manageable at that point – I sat separately from my boyfriend, so was less distracted – but German was attuned to my personality in some way. I liked the way it felt to speak its hard and soft sounds; I liked that it kept to its rules. French and Spanish were so fluid and flamboyant, whereas German felt stable and subdued. I was also fascinated by this place that seemed so much better than ours, *Vorsprung durch Technik*, but that had a past so taboo no one could mention World War II or the Nazis. I wanted to know what had happened, how they had apparently redeemed themselves, if they had.

Shortly after handing in my selection form, the school announced that languages would not be offered due to lack of funding, capacity and interest. A painfully quiet sixteen-year-old me went to the staff room to beg – *please, please* – for them not to cancel them. Eventually, three teachers agreed to teach me and a couple more students ad hoc over two years in what was called 'the broom cupboard' – a tiny room at the end of the Languages corridor. The other students dropped their languages after the first year, but I continued. I was the only student doing any language at A-level and was taking two. It was just me having the odd one-on-one with these poor overworked teachers.

One day, out of the blue, my German teacher (who had actually lived in Germany! And used to be married to a German man!) brought in the first page of Franz Kafka's *Die Verwandlung* (*The Metamorphosis*) for me to try and read, which was a leap from what I was able to do at that point. During that first exposure to literature in a foreign language in that cupboard room with my German teacher, I remember realising:

books are written in other languages;

this is like trying to read a poem I don't yet understand;

there's a story inside this, I wonder what it is.

I got a mid-B in German in the end, nothing spectacular. It didn't even occur to me to apply to study languages at university, and no one encouraged me to. Better to stick with English.

The *Frankfurter Allgemeine Zeitung*, the German-language newspaper usually simply called FAZ, published a piece about the German author Michael Kleeberg calling for better pay for literary translators. Our cleaning staff have this quote printed on their dust cloths, there's one hanging off the broom: 'The fact that a profession that requires a profound knowledge of a language, linguistic sensitivity, and creative potential, in which it takes years to achieve real expertise, is paid like a cleaner's job, is a scandal everyone should stand up against.'

Maybe the scandal isn't simply that literary translators get paid like cleaners, but that cleaners and translators both get paid unfairly.

While translator-in-residence at a large institution, I interviewed the multilingual staff to research how they used their languages in official and unofficial ways. It was imperative to me that this didn't include only the curatorial staff – those working in the winding corridors behind doors, often hired and paid to be experts in different languages and world regions – but the information desk staff, the security staff and catering staff, the cleaning staff – people who were front of house, who spoke to visitors every day in multiple languages as a matter of course, most of whom were not paid to offer multilingual assistance. They were just visible, and therefore called upon to help. I had to ask permission from external companies who managed the catering and the security to feature their employees, but the cleaning company wouldn't give me permission to feature the cleaning staff, to make these (unofficial) linguists visible.

OK, everybody out. Take that apron off and put it back, please.
    Watch out for the bucket and mop on your way out.

Miniature Railway

All aboard!

First stop, My Family Home (a model of it at the side of the track, it's even pebble-dashed). Have you got German family? My dad is Maltese, my mum was Anglo-Irish, but I can speak none of my heritage languages apart from English. My parents believed it would be confusing to learn languages other than English. This lack created a void.

Next stop, Munich. I remember having a faltering conversation with a boy I was going home with from a club who queried why I didn't know quite a simple German word for something, yet knew the word Gleis/train platform. Waiting for trains and riding them was when there was a pause, a time when I could read the billboards and adverts running over the seats like pages from textbooks, with their helpful text-and-image layouts, and listen to the looping language-learning cassette of train announcements and the advanced listening exam of passenger conversation.

Willa Muir talks about how she and her husband <u>Edwin Muir</u> learnt Czech through guesswork while living in Prague in 1921–22:

> As soon as we got out of the train in the large station, a mathematically symmetrical station, we were faced by identical stairways at either end. One stairway was marked Vchod, the other Vychod; thus we began to learn the only practical method of discovering Prague, through our foot-soles, through our skins, through our noses as much as through our eyes.

Next stop, A Split in the Track. When I rarely do speak German in the UK, my mind is constantly fighting it, I can feel the wires overheating, it makes me regress to being a teenager. Since I spend every day working from German to English, one way, doing the creating and expressing in English made from German, it can feel difficult to create German from scratch. When I bump into a young German woman who lives locally, I forget how to speak German and she soon switches to English, concerned by my lack of German (today, when I bumped into her again, instead of saying *Macht nichts*, it doesn't matter, I said *Macht kein Sinn*, it doesn't make any sense).

It's like having to make a piece of art with unfamiliar materials or writing using my left hand, nothing comes out the way I want it to.

I get asked if I write in German, if I translate myself into German. I know German *so well*, we're intimately befriended (sounds like the German word befreundet, to be friends). If German were a person, I could profile them and tell you everything about them, but I couldn't impersonate or be them. I just don't know German in that way, it's not our relationship.

Let's take the right-hand track, the one that has a sign saying: *Why did you move to Munich when you were eighteen?*

That's easy, I obviously moved to Germany on my own when I was eighteen so I could improve my German – oh, this journey's a little bumpy, why's it juddering. I wanted to be exposed to a different culture – woah, the carriages are swaying. I – I moved to Munich because, well, erm, I was very independent and was always heading off on adventures.

Oh, we've wound up in a siding by the fire exit. That wasn't meant to happen. Everybody off.

Fire Exit

The exit signs here are purple neon, not green. You probably assumed that they would be green, because they're always green.

For many years I convinced myself that I had moved to Munich for the obvious reasons: language, travel, gap year. The truth eventually rose to the surface a couple of years ago while I was on a translation residency. I had moved to Munich because I wanted to move out of home, create distance between me and my parents, and get away from my long-term boyfriend. Someone gave me an opportunity to leave that just happened to be in Munich, Germany.

I had found the last few years of living at home very difficult, and felt conflicted about the relationship I'd been in since I was fourteen. Then a former student from my school, Katie, who was perhaps six or seven years older and who had moved to Munich after university, came to visit. She said to our sixth form group, perhaps in a more offhand way than I heard it, that if anyone wanted to come and stay with her for a bit to experience Germany they should contact her.

A light went on in my head and I immediately said I wanted to go and stay, and in my mind I knew that I was moving away for a long time. Two months later, after my A-levels were done, I was in Katie's flat, having dragged a huge suitcase through the snow, without a thick winter coat and with big holes in my jeans. I stayed with her for two weeks, maybe three weeks, maybe even four. I went to an interview at a job agency and waited for job offers, using up my time not realising I should be helping with the cooking, the cleaning, the shopping, and instead wandering around the city and sleeping in late. I don't know how Katie put up with this sullen teenager encroaching on her space.

The interview at the agency Katie had recommended had been painful to get through, the man at the office had to point at the calendar on the wall behind him, speaking German loudly and slowly.

I was in a daze, and cried the first few nights. I had never been away from home for this long, I had left behind my friends, my boyfriend, my family. But I had done it because I was desperate. I was so anxious and dependent that although I could drive, I had never taken a bus or a train on my own, and I feared that, if I stayed in my home town any longer, I would stay there forever, stay with my boyfriend out of ease, keep living with my parents, go more and more inside myself.

Eventually I got a job as an au pair and moved out and really started my life abroad. Katie had got me into the country, she had smuggled me out of dangerous territory.

This will be your last chance to leave the Fair, it takes you straight to the gift shop (p. 200).

TALK: My Life as an Au Pair in Munich

MOVED TO AN EXTERNAL VENUE

B9 – Bed Time

Here is a darkened room filled with different places to sleep, each with a plinth next to it. I think it must be inspired by Tracey Emin's *My Bed*, which was one of the first pieces of art I saw in a gallery as a teenager.

Mattress of Epiphany

First, there's a mattress; you can sit on it if you want. You don't have to, but I'd like you to sit with me on it. This mattress is in the attic of a property owned by the landlord who promised me and my friends that a house would be ready the summer we moved out of student halls. It wasn't. Three of us are on mattresses in the hot loft conversion of one of his other houses, two of us are in the annex in the garden.

On this short plinth next to my mattress is a special artefact, the first novel I ever read in German: *Der Vorleser* by Bernhard Schlink. A smooth, white paperback, typical of the publisher Diogenes, first released in 1995. I chose it at random in a chain bookshop when I lived in Munich aged eighteen, nineteen. I liked the cover – a detail from a painting by Ernst Ludwig Kirchner of Nollendorfplatz that looks like an X, a warped, fish-eyed gaze on a crossroads in dirty yellow and grey-blue. That's the original painting, on the wall to the right of the mattress. In my first year at university, I was nocturnal and would often miss my 9 a.m. lectures in English literature, but would then be up late trying to decipher poems by Erich Kästner in a little yellow book (it's hidden behind the Schlink on the plinth), it was like reading in 4D, interpretation with interpretation on top. I wanted to try to read something longer.

Let's take *Der Vorleser* down and try to read it. Let's ignore the books I should be reading for the second year of my undergrad degree in English.

In spite of living in Munich for nearly a year before university, and an additional three months when I was Munich-sick the following summer, the one I've just returned from, my German is still bad. Everyone I associated with pretty much only spoke to me in English. I worked in an English-speaking office. Before that I had been an au pair for a wealthy family and they had forbidden me from speaking anything other than English with their kids. I had absorbed some of the language, it had improved, but I couldn't really say how.

This is what I can make out from the first page. Up on the wall over there, that first blown-up photocopy, it's a little wrinkly from the wheat paste:

> When I fifteen was, had I   The illness
> began in the autumn and ended in spring. Colder and
> darker the old year became,   weaker became I.
> First with the new year went it   The January was
> warm, and my mother   me the bed on the
> balcony. I saw the heavens, the sun, the clouds and
> heard the children in the yard play. An early evening in
> February heard I a   sing.

or, version two, on that wall over there:

> When I was fifteen, I had [insert an illness]. The illness
> began in the autumn and ended in the spring. The colder and
> darker the old year became [or got], the weaker I got [or became].
> It [I guess 'improved'?] only with the start of the new year. January was
> warm, and my mother [moved? set up?] the bed on the
> balcony. I saw the [sky? 'Himmel' must mean heaven *and* sky?], the
>   sun, the clouds and
> heard the children in the yard. One early evening in
> February I heard a [insert a bird] sing [or singing?].

I'm stunned, and, unusually for me, excited. This is so much more than I had managed when trying to read the first page of Franz Kafka's *The Metamorphosis* with my A-level teacher two years earlier.

The first chapter of Part 1 of *Der Vorleser* is just over two pages long. I manage to read it, about the boy who lived on Blumenstrasse (Flower Street!) walking into Bahnhofstrasse (Station Street!) and being sick in the street, then helped by a woman whose first move is to get him to slosh buckets of water to clean away the vomit, who holds him when he starts to cry and then takes him home. In a few lines she goes from being a stern stranger to an object of desire through her hug where her breasts (Brüste) press against his chest (Brust) and the detail that he was '[blank] taller than her' – barely taller – but taller nonetheless! An intriguing dynamic is formed from one moment to the next. In the last few lines of this opening, he says that his mother told him to buy her flowers, introduce himself to her (I can read this now) and thank her. The last line – which draws me in completely with its abruptness and holding back – is, 'So I went, at the end of February, to the Bahnhofstrasse.'

It will take me about nine months to get through the whole thing. Sometimes I'll use a dictionary, other times I'll let my eyes run over the lines and fill in massive holes in my knowledge with imagination. How would they go from here to there? What would she say to him if he said that to her? How might he react at this point? Looking at this first page now, it feels so strange to know how I would translate it, how only I would translate it. Even stranger to think that now I pick up novels in German, open them, read them, and know how to translate them into books you buy in shops. That people trust me to do this.

We eventually move into a house, with actual beds, and I continue seeking out German and translation. I write an essay on the aesthetics of Kraftwerk and Rammstein, and a trio of essays for one module about Antonioni's *Blow-Up* (an adaptation of a short story by Julio Cortázar), Vladimir Nabokov and Russian émigré identity translated into film, and the films of Werner Herzog. A year after I finish my undergrad degree, I start a master's in German Studies, but it all started as a sneaky sideline and thread through my English degree.

Bed Sleuth

A double bed with a floral duvet that smells of my/your parents.

I remember being home with the flu from school once and being allowed to rest in my parents' big bed. I read Philip Pullman's *The Amber Spyglass*, which I'd borrowed from a friend. A key object in the series *His Dark Materials* is the alethiometer. It's similar to a large pocket watch, but instead of numbers there are symbols around its face, and three hands. When the main protagonist Lyra needs an answer to a question, she consults the alethiometer, and its hands move to land on three symbols at a time. She then instinctively knows how to interpret these three standalone pictures to form an answer. This is similar to when I started translating; I would have to cling on to one or two words or images and see how they related to one another and fill in the gaps. It was like learning to read all over again, linking a series of disparate images or moments to create something whole and fluid. I often say translating for me is intuitive, instinctual, but I don't mean that it's automatic or unchallenging – it's more that I have to sink into a space of being open, allowing associations to flicker before my mind's eye, often trusting myself to find connections, while checking myself when it comes a little too easily or while not concentrating.

I sometimes open a book in German just to check whether I really can read German, surprised every time when a story starts playing before my mind's eye. I sometimes open a book in English just to see what happens, shocked when, yes, I read the words and they activate, begin to fizz into sensations and ideas.

Another time, while ill on holiday, I watched the film version of Dan Brown's infamous *The Da Vinci Code*. The cryptologist played by Tom Hanks can look at an anagram, a phrase or series of numbers and unpick the puzzle. In the film, we see through his eyes as the pertinent parts of what he's looking at light up or float above the writing in blood or on a painting to show us the order he sees in his mind. I find having a visual mind helps me when I decipher a text, parts glow in different colours, they have different textures, I just know in myself what feels right.

Purple sleeping bags arranged on the floor in the centre of the room next to a folded-out sofa bed.

When I was in my early teens I went to a local amateur theatre group. I went with my best friend Abby, who was the same age as me and lived next door. We made friends with a girl at the group called E. We all bonded over Harry Potter, and I remember we had a sleepover at E's when we were about fourteen or fifteen where we stayed up all night collaboratively writing a new Harry Potter book. We had read and reread these books so closely that we knew the characters, how they would speak, what they would say, and knew the style of the books inside and out. We ate snacks, snuggled in our sleeping bags, discussing and transcribing the collaborative book all through the night.

A couple of years later, I would have regular sleepovers with my friend Helen round my house, where we would watch two or three films a night and one or two the next day, and would have a running commentary volleying between us all the way through them, analysing (and snorting or swooning at) the dialogue – we still quote the worst and best lines at each other in person or over text. We could hear what was cringey, what lacked authenticity.

A few years ago, I started a small press for Maltese literature with my friend Kat Storace. Kat and I have always lived far from one another; me in London, her in Oxfordshire, me in Hastings, her in Nairobi, me in Hastings, her in Paris. When it's time to read submissions or edit a manuscript, we sometimes have an open Zoom call so we feel like we're together. Last year, we were able to actually be together while doing the final proofreading of a novel and an anthology we were publishing. I came to stay at her place, an annex on the side of a house she was renting in the countryside outside Banbury. We sat side by side, proofing page after page, crunching on snacks. Kat accidently knocked a cup of tea over the novel print-out and we had to run around, swearing and laughing, hanging the pages of the manuscript over the radiators and chairs in her house until they dried as it was our only copy. We edited late into the evening and then got into our pyjamas to eat dinner, watch TV and discuss the day's collaborative edit.

My Bed

This one most closely resembles Emin's *My Bed*. It's a recreation of my bed in my room in a Wohngemeinschaft (WG) in Munich, a flat with strangers with a shared bathroom and no kitchen, just a hotplate in each room. There are cartons of warm juice under the bed, half a jar of Nutella within reach, stale bedclothes. There were cheap paperbacks of English classics in the same chain bookshop I picked up *Der Vorleser* in, and I finally started to read books I hadn't had access to at home or at school: *Frankenstein, Peter Pan, Alice's Adventures in Wonderland*. It felt like reading a foreign language; they were challenging and needed focus and attention to get through. After reading *Alice*, I bought a dual-language edition, one page in English, one in German, as I thought it might help my German skills. But I soon realised it wasn't going to be straightforward. Even the words I did know in German didn't match up when I checked the English side. The parts that rhymed did rhyme, but seemed to be saying different things. There was a glossary in the back to explain English quirks and references. It wasn't a dictionary, it was a literary translation, reaching for things like effect and sound. I spent lots of time alone in this room, making my way through my books, but I also wasn't always alone.

When it was apparent that the Erasmus programme was being killed off due to Brexit, a journalist for a right-wing newspaper wrote a piece about how it was nothing more than a student sex holiday. When I moved of my own accord to Germany when I was eighteen, a big motivator for getting better at the language turned out to be desire. I couldn't perceive my German improving, but after three months, I was at a house party talking to someone I fancied and realised I was speaking in German. I was actually testing out my new German skills while also trying out my brand-new flirtation skills. Michel Foucault tells an anecdote of becoming an intellectual because he wanted to impress a boy he fancied at school. We are pushed by such motivations, at least initially.

But it wasn't just for purposes of seduction, it was making friends in general, being able to joke, connect, communicate, make plans, ask questions.

There's an Anglo-German organisation that tries to foster the will among English students to learn German, and they often lead with the idea in their Facebook posts that it will make them more attractive in the job market. They really need to lead with: you could meet people, sleep with them, fall in and out of love with them, be lifelong friends with them, and the language.

Fucking as Research

A comfy double bed with two single duvets (as is the way in Germany).

I'm currently a member of a Facebook forum for translators from any language into German. Though I translate from German into English, I like to see what issues translators have with English texts. I think it might be useful for my own writing, but I'm just curious really. There's a cross-stitch over the bed displaying a quote from Morgan Giles explaining that part of the reason for her learning Japanese is because she's nosy and loves gossip, next to another cross-stitch showing a quote from a piece in *Poets & Writers*: 'Authors need to become better allies and learn what translators need and desire.'

Friederike von Criegern posted in the Facebook group saying that she had to share some excerpts from a recent correspondence she'd had with a distant relative who had shown interest in a book she had translated.

I'm happy to translate for you:

If I may say something about the book itself, it has less to do with you than with the author. It's regarding the obscenities with which the reader is constantly confronted. Does one have to be exposed to the most intimate shenanigans down to the last detail? Does this have any literary value? And if I may be a bit cheeky: Did you have to actively carry out all these shenanigans yourself in order to be able to translate them correctly?

Uh, YES, OF COURSE!, Friederike writes under the message. *Method translation! And you can all be happy that it was just sex and that I don't translate detective stories!*

Bedtime Story

A small, cold double bed next to a draughty window (a hole in the wall with a fan running through it).

I like making people laugh, it was always my defence mechanism as a weird and solitary kid, and I was brought up in a dryly funny and sarcastic household and on late-night TV comedy shows. I like delivering a joke or an anecdote well, coming up with a pun and seeing people's faces light up, or triggering their laughter. I can get frustrated when people tell stories or jokes badly – rushing them, flunking how they start or end, not hitting the beats to make them land. I really knew I wanted to translate fiction when I was reading the second ever book I'd read in German one night in bed, laughed out loud, felt compelled to live-translate the section to my then-boyfriend-now-partner Richard, and he laughed too. I'd done that. The author and I had done that – what a double act.

Nap

Here's a sofa and a blanket. Sometimes I'm so exhausted from translating I have to take a nap, or a few days where I stare at the TV to wipe my brain.

D7/C7 – Busts of Willa Muir and Anthea Bell

Here on the outer corner between two stands is a bust of Willa Muir, and beside it one of Anthea Bell, translators of many prominent German-language writers. You can listen to them speaking on the headphones hanging beneath their terracotta likenesses, which have wildflowers growing from their scalps.

Muir was born Wilhelmina Anderson in Montrose, Scotland, to Shetlandic parents in 1890. She wrote a memoir of her marriage to her husband and fellow translator Edwin Muir called *Belonging*, which is just as much a memoir about translation. Muir describes working on translations nearly a hundred years ago, in Hampstead in the 1930s, the decade of Anthea Bell's birth:

> After some argument we had jacked up our fee for translation to two guineas a thousand [words], which was supposed to be very good pay, but many hours of hard work were needed to earn a sizeable sum.

> We had no royalty on the book's sales; we got only our translation fee of £250, and seemed always to be paying out another three guineas for Press clippings. It was the publishers who raked in the thousands.

> Yet there was always a press of work, and so I reverted to a student habit of mine, working at furious speed late at night into the small hours, after the vibrations of the day had died down. During the summers I sat up all night once in a while, hearing the birds sing at dawn and tumbling into bed for a few hours' sleep after breakfast, but I did this only when a translation had to be finished in a hurry or proofs corrected against a deadline.

Things haven't changed that much since then. Translators are still underpaid and overworked, few royalties are secured, some publishers make huge profits off translators' work. But the Muirs could at least earn a living (with underwhelming pay negotiations) from a few translations and Edwin infrequently reviewing novels, and they could live in London (Hampstead was a bohemian place back then). Though Muir talks of the costs of having a child, they can afford a nanny and part of the household being taken care of by a maid. I had to move out of London four years ago because I could never do enough translations to earn a living. Writing a book review earns me five per cent of my monthly costs.

No books were written by or about Anthea Bell, who was born in Suffolk and read English at Oxford; her father was *The Times* newspaper's first crossword setter, her son is a journalist. She did write a few essays that are enlightening about her work translating authors like W. G. Sebald:

> These days a translator usually corresponds with an author by email, but Max Sebald did not like computer technology, and indeed claimed, with a humorous glint in his eye, that when a computer was delivered to his room at the University of East Anglia it stayed in its box, still packed. So we corresponded by old-fashioned snail mail, Max in his beautiful handwriting, I typing my letters because it is unkind to ask anyone to read my writing, as we discussed various points of translation back and forth.

The summer after I finished my postgrad, during which I had become obsessed with the idea of literary translation – at least, that is, the idea of using German and creative writing together – I applied to do a week-long residential course on literary translation. I was offered a place, and my request for a grant to cover most of the costs was successful. The week was taught by Maureen Freely and Sasha Dugdale, with guests Daniel Hahn and also *the* Anthea Bell. I remember Anthea talking about how she would sometimes need to write up a translation on a typewriter and send the only copy of the manuscript by post across the ocean to America, and that she was an early adopter of technology, mastering computers while editors presumed she was a Luddite or technophobe due to her age.

During that course, I went from only surmising what translation is – words exchanged into other words – to what I know now: translation is literature I've understood utterly and completely rewritten into literature.

Sasha Dugdale, after I tried 'translating' a poem by Paul Celan: 'Do you actually know what this poem *means*?' (I did not.)

Maureen Freely, after I redrafted an attempt at translating a few hundred words from a novel: 'You've got it! A translation of a story is a *story*.'

I would go on to work with Anthea when I edited *New Books in German* magazine; she was on the editorial committee. She was always working on a translation and knew so much about German-language literature. She was funny and charming, and a great translator. The other day I saw an article about Sebald that quoted freely from one of her translations, and she isn't mentioned anywhere. I'm mentioning her here.

If only we had an autobiography or biography of Anthea. I'm going to imagine it was on its way here and fell into the sea outside.

G5 – Hall of Mirrors (Reflections on a Sentence)

A Translation Duel is when two or more translators gently compete by comparing their translations of the same extract of a novel or the same poem in front of a live audience at a book fair or literary festival. This scenario allows them to show how and why they made their decisions, and to demonstrate how different these decisions may end up being between two exceptional translators. At the end of the hour, when barely a few lines have been examined, a winner is sometimes declared, but it's nearly always pronounced a draw by the moderator.

In the Hall of Mirrors, the translation duel is between a translator and their many selves – the duel that goes on in their mind, with other shades of self, even before they meet an editor, or reader, or another translator brandishing their versions – and it is intense, agonising, stressful. It feels like a matter of life and death.

You press this button, here, on the outside of the booth, and a slip of paper comes out of this slit (try to ignore the grubby hand shoving it out). On the piece of paper is a paragraph from a novel or a poem or a few lines from a play, with the line you need to translate underlined. Then, after a few stretches, you step inside the mirrored room, like so.

Allow me to demonstrate. Here I am, refracted into my most querying self, my most enthusiastic self, a pragmatic self, a wild self, my tired self, my most unsure self, but also a well-prepared self, an unprepared self, a distracted self, and so on.

See: I have been instructed to translate the first line of Marion Poschmann's novel *Die Kieferninseln*, or *The Pine Islands*.

The timer has started running, but we don't know how long we've got. Time behaves strangely in here anyway.

Er hatte geträumt, dass seine Frau ihn betrog.

| *He had dreamt that his wife had been unfaithful.*
| Dreamed? Dreamt?
| Dreamt. No, dreamed?
| And there are two 'hads', which seems like too many.
| You don't need a 'had' bit for the 'unfaithful' part in German, but you do in English.
| Just: 'his wife was unfaithful', surely?
| But then she would have written 'dass seine Frau untreu war'.
| Was being unfaithful?
| See, that sounds clunky to me.
| Do we need the 'had' before 'dreamt'? 'Dreamt' kind of implies the had without having a had?
| But 'dreamt' looks like the present tense somehow.
| But it's not.
| But it looks like it is.
| I just got an alert on my phone! It's from the Hall of Mirrors: *Don't forget! Translators get paid per word, not by the hour!*
| How could I forget.
| He had been dreaming.
| What?
| He had been dreaming that his wife…
| I mean, sure. But also, 'had been' really slows down the sentence; it's meant to be short and snappy.
| He had a dream. (I have a dream!)
| It doesn't say 'He had a dream', otherwise it would be 'Er hatte einen Traum'. And it's also in the past tense, so it would be 'He had had a dream'.
| Obviously I wouldn't put 'He had had', I'd put 'He'd had a dream', I'm not a monstrous pest.
| So maybe we could use 'He'd been dreaming'?
| I like that.
| But wouldn't that be more 'Er träumte'?
| Wow, only thousands of sentences to go.

| And what about 'he'd been daydreaming'?
| What!
| What?
| The next line says he woke up. In bed. He can't be daydreaming. And to daydream is *tag*träumen – to *day*dream.
| Just thought it could be a bit more out there. A reverie?
| Well, he literally wakes up in the next line.
| *As Gregor Samsa awoke one morning from uneasy dreams, he found himself transformed...* this line is absolutely a Kafka reference!
| No, stop.
| The dreamer is called Gilbert Silvester! G.S.! Gregor Samsa! He wakes up transformed after dreams!
| Oh God.
| Which Kafka translation are you quoting from, though?
| Do you even know how many people have translated *The Metamorphosis*?
| You mean *Die Verwandlung*!
| You're not impressing anybody by doing that.
| Too many.
| Not enough.
| Oh wow, turns out a lot.
| That's the Willa and Edwin Muir one, the first translation, from 1933.
| *After uneasy dreams that his wife...*
| But there's also 'troubled dreams' (Hofmann, 2007)
| *After troubled dreams that his wife...*
| ...'agitated dreams' (Neugroschel, 1993)
| *After agitated dreams that his wife...*
| ...'unsettling dreams' (Corngold, 1972)
| *After unsettling dreams that his wife...*
| That's before even getting to the bug bit.
| Shouldn't we be looking at the original Kafka line, not the translations?
| *Als Gregor Samsa eines Morgens aus unruhigen Träumen erwachte, fand er sich in seinem Bett zu einem ungeheueren Ungeziefer verwandelt.*
| If I were translating it today, I'd probably go with: 'When Gregor

Samsa awoke one morning from uneasy dreams, he found himself in his bed transformed into a monstrous pest.' But that's just one line of Kafka…

| That might actually be underestimating the potential of 'unruhig'.
| 'Anxious'.
| A bit millennial.
| 'Unruhig' with regard to sleep is apparently 'restless' or 'fitful'.
| 'Turbulent', 'gumplefik' [Scot.] [archaic].
| I wouldn't worry about it too much, I don't think you'll be retranslating Kafka anytime soon.
| Can we verify that it's a reference somehow? Is there anything online, in an interview or review somewhere?
| I'll check on my phone.
| Should we ask the author?
| I could WhatsApp her?
| Won't she think we've gone loopy? It's only the first line of the book. She won't find that very reassuring.
| Just ask her how she would translate it and we can get this over and done with…
| And every other line.
| I just got another alert: the author just asked if we've finished the translation yet. Oh, and the publisher wants an early peek. And the book cover designer needs us to write a blurb ASAP.
| First lines are important though. They can become iconic, or reference iconic opening ones.
| I mean, we should pay attention to the literary history and context of the book.
| But would that really change anything? Anything we've already been doing?
| Readers might not get the reference even if we did implant it in there somehow.
| They might naturally make the same connection that we did anyway.
| Fundamentally, Poschmann's original line looks nothing like Kafka's line, it definitely doesn't have anything about Gregor having a wife and her cheating on him.

| Hang on, *cheating on him*, not 'unfaithful'?
| Well, firstly, we haven't included the *him*, *ihn*, element up to now.
| It didn't seem that important.
| Secondly, unfaithful sounds very Victorian.
| Well, I've read the whole book, and he's a quite old-world kind of guy, Gilbert.
| Oh, I haven't read it yet.
| I like translating having not read the book, it keeps it exciting.
| That's cute.
| And sometimes there's not enough time to read it first.
| But hang on, just because he's an old-fashioned kind of guy, it doesn't mean the narrator is.
| That's a good point.
| And anyway, 'unfaithful' is also kind of ambiguous?
| I think you'd get what it meant.
| Isn't it a good thing that it's slightly ambiguous?
| I think if you use a 'He'd' you could use a 'cheated', but if it's 'He had' it would go best with 'unfaithful', they fit together.
| How?
| In terms of the register and the feel.
| Has anyone actually looked up 'betrog'?
| It's obviously 'cheated', etc.
| 'betrog', jd. betrog, jemanden betrog, to betrog *someone*, can mean...
| ...deceived somebody...
| ...tricked sb...
| ...swindled sb...
| ...jockeyed, defrauded...
| Ha, it can mean 'trepanned somebody'.
| 'He had dreamt that his wife had trepanned him', that would be such a great opening for a thriller.
| Shit, but none of them directly means 'cheated'? So it should be 'deceived him'?
| 'Betrog' is the past tense, look up 'betrügen', to...
| 'Betrügen' and 'betrog' makes me think of 'lügen' and 'log' as in 'to lie' and 'lied'...

| A German Lied, get it?
| Please don't do that.
| Plus a German did lie, didn't she, so it's actually true as well as a joke.
| No, he *dreamt* – dreamed?! – that she had.
| Betrügen: 'To deceive, to cheat somebody' – not specifically to cheat *on* somebody – 'to betray'...
| You know, 'betrog' sounds like 'betray', maybe it's been staring us in the face the whole time.
| Well, 'geträumt' sounds like 'dreamt', but look how far we got with that.
| It's a bit melodramatic, isn't it? You betrayed me! You deceived me!
| But it's literature, it's dramatic.
| ...'to defraud, to scam, to con'...
| It's all very monetary, transactional...
| Maybe she stole money from him, maybe it's 'He'd dreamt his wife had been conning him out of money'?
| Like I said, I read it, it's not that. A couple of pages in it says 'He'd clear the way. For whoever it was.' Something like that anyway, a discussion for another time.
| New alert: another publisher wants to know if we could translate another book very soon and have it finished about the same time as this current book. They want to know now. And whether we could lower our rate. Perfect.
| Looks like 'deceived him' is the best option.
| Don't you mean 'had been deceiving him'? It's not *had* betrog*ged* him, it's had been betrog*ging* him, continuously over time.
| I hadn't finished, by the way: 'to beguile, to fool, to dupe, to swindle'... Ooo, *to cuckold!*
| Cuckold!
| If we're not having 'unfaithful', we're not having 'cuckolded'.
| 'Had been cuckolding...'
| Hang on, right at the bottom in the dictionary there's 'to cheat on sb (wife, boyfriend, etc.)'.
| Wife, boyfriend? Why not 'wife, husband'? That's not very consistent.

| We're skipping over the fact that Frau means wife, but also woman, right?
| You're losing it.
| We shouldn't just dismiss 'his woman had been cheating…', there's something in that.
| No one would like a narrator who said that.
| 'to two-time'.
| 'She's been two-timing me with that two-timing son o' a bitch!'
| Yeah, sticking with the American theme, there's also 'step out on'.
| 'to be unfaithful to sb (e.g. a spouse)'.
| That's where we started.
| Just out of interest, can we flip it, what is under 'to cheat on'?
| Betrügen.
| Ha.
| Or 'fremdgehen', but that's more colloquial, apparently. 'Going other' or, yes, 'playing away' would be a nice equivalent, that's satisfying.
| To be unfaithful to somebody?
| Betrügen.
| So we have to decide.
| I say 'unfaithful', it has depth.
| I say 'cheated on', it's snappier. It just doesn't need so much bumpf around it. '… that his wife *had been being* unfaithful to him.'
| That's a bit extreme, we obviously wouldn't do that.
| 'That his wife had been unfaithful to him', 'that his wife had cheated on him'. It's hard.
| Do we need the 'that'?
| Do we need the 'that'?!
| 'To him', 'on him' – can we cut that and just have 'had been cheating', 'had been unfaithful'?
| Maybe with the latter, not with the former.
| It does say 'ihn', though, 'to him'.
| You, the one who actually read the book, does this line come up again anywhere else in the book? Like, verbatim or adapted? Does he have more dreams, how are they written about? We should be consistent, or consider being consistent?

| I mean, I think you need to have read the whole book to even know how to approach the first sentence. Any sentence. Otherwise it's out of context.
| Very insightful, but we need something *now*.
| Did we decide about the dreaming part? Or about the 'that'?
| Do we need to talk about the comma?
| Are you joking?
| The comma is only there because it's a convention to have one before 'dass' in German, it's got nothing to do with anything.
| But what if it's trying to tell us something?
| I wonder how someone else would do it...

OK, there's the buzzer, lights up, let's get out, I need some air.

Please write your translation in the space provided at the bottom of your piece of paper and submit it through the slit in the wall:

....

If you would like to translate the next sentence, please press the number 2 now.

If you would like to go up against a rival translator, please press the number 3 now.

If you would like to go up against two rival translators, please press the number 4 now.

If you would like to go up against three or more (max. fifteen) rival translators, please press the number 5 now.

By submitting your translation, you will automatically be entered into a competition to win a commission to translate the whole novel.

S6 – Custard Pies

Lock me in the stocks! Five custard pies to the face; one for each heckle I've received at a panel discussion about literary translation.

Pastel green pie incoming – *SPLAT!* Once the green sludge has slipped from my face, I see that inside the shed foil pie casing on the floor are the words:

Being a full-time literary translator is selfish!

A few years ago, I received a long email out of the blue from some-one I didn't know, asking if I would mentor them on a poetry trans-lation project. The email set out how much they wanted to translate the poet and the closeness they felt to the work, the events they had been attending to gain knowledge about literary translation, and that they had received funding to work on the project. They asked if I would meet them for a coffee for forty-five minutes so they could 'ask as many questions' as they 'could fit in' the very next day, or in a week's time at a precise time, about an hour's travel from where I lived, so I could instruct them in how to approach the translation as they'd never translated poetry before.

I congratulated them on the funding and offered to meet them and/or take a look at their translations to offer comments or editing, and that I could do this for £60 an hour. I couldn't afford to take time out of my working week, I explained. I also privately thought: I've built up my skills as a translator, including poetry translation, and asking for payment reflects the time I've invested in learning this skill. And if they have received funding, paying me for a little of my time seems fair. They replied in two lines that they would look into other avenues, and that was that.

Later that year I took part in a panel discussion, and during the Q&A, myself and the other panellists – all of us literary translators – were asked whether a translator had to do promotional events and other side work for free (my response was along the lines of: if you want to). After we had given our answers, a member of the audience said that maybe literary translators should get full-time jobs and translate on the side, so doing events or answering questions for emerging translators – looking pointedly at me – could be done for free. I realised that it was the person who had emailed me.

While taking part in a Zoom meeting for a cultural organisation looking to learn more about mentoring schemes, I talked about why I started mentoring independently: that the first time I mentored it was a commission from the British Council and the London Book Fair, and the experience made me realise I had knowledge and skills I could share; that I received enquiries for mentoring or for 'pick your brains coffees' quite frequently; that because of my experience of D.I.Y. culture I could just Do-It-Myself by announcing on Twitter that I could offer low-cost mentorships (no application process) and one free mentorship each time I opened my books – about once every six months – to someone who couldn't afford it, or someone from an underrepresented background in literary translation.

After I'd given my short talk, one of the other translator-mentors who was invited to speak, and who had a part-time job, said that they were always happy to meet people for coffees and offer advice for free, as they thought it was a nice thing to do and enjoyed helping people.

Once the event was over, I felt slightly ashamed. It's mean not to work for free, was the message. That's not very generous, that's not very punk. (I recall the 'opportunities' to play actual punk shows where no fee would be offered and the promoter would get all proceeds from the ticket sales, and when we'd say we would need money even just to cover our costs, like travel and food, we would be told we were 'not punk'.) All this illustrates the idea that the issue is money – if you ask for money, even if the person asking you for something gains financially, or in terms of knowledge or skilled work, you are not a good person. And more than that, you're not a good *artist*.

Should I have kept my full- or part-time jobs so I could always mentor people for free? Would that make me a better translator? Better person?

No. That's not for me. That's not what I have chosen.

When I had full-time and part-time jobs, it meant I didn't have the time or energy to translate and write as well as I could, or to do enough work to hone my skills. It also made me less likely to ask for fees that reflected the actual work that translating books entailed and the skills I had as a translator – perpetuating the low fees translators receive.

There are translators who could afford, financially and time-wise, to give free mentorships and advice, but I can't. Or rather, I would take small payments – from £75 for two hours of discussion and my feedback on a thousand words of a translation – that would also go towards paying for the free twelve-hour mentorship I offered. There are translators far more experienced than me who wouldn't or couldn't give mentorships and advice even if you paid them, because they don't want to or have too much actual translation work to do. It was a decision to add mentoring to my portfolio. Do I think trainee translators should have to front the cost of training? I don't know, I'm just one person offering to mentor people in my field, because it's what I can do right now. I often get asked whether translating full-time is possible. I wonder if the translator who wants my time for free has the aim of translating full-time?

I get to decide when I work for free, and I get to decide if something is worthwhile for me to do, paid or otherwise. I have a metric for it. Can I just hand these out? Sorry if there's custard on them.

The artist Ima-Abasi Okon created an installation at The Showroom in London called *General Service Agreement* (2018), which explores artist time, labour, pay and so on in the form and style of a contract and questionnaire that could be sent to a client enquiring after your services.

It lays down the parameters and realities of a project-based artist in such a professional and confident way – one that is ubiquitous in 'regular' professions, but in the context of an artist seems shocking, jarring, confusing, almost strangely humorous. I find this document genius in the way it expresses the unsaid aspects of freelance creatives' labour and the frequent taking advantage of its intangibility by individuals and organisations. Okon sets down in writing that an artist should have the same working week and overtime at weekends that many other kinds of jobs offer, and also sets out clear pay bands and day rates for different levels of experience held by artists in their lives and careers.

Clauses in the agreement include:

2. PAYMENT

[...]

c) By 'payment' this agreement means: it will never be enough, because human relations are always in excess of their quantification, and we need both to be together and to sustain ourselves.

[...]

4. RESPONSIBILITIES

[...]

c) Be as kind as we are capable of being.

The questionnaire section of the artwork/agreement is a radical tool that also confirms and validates my experience. It gives a framework to facilitate my living and working that I have a hunch is right for me. The questionnaire is to be completed by the 'Artist' to help them decide whether an 'Opportunity' is to be accepted based on new criteria.

For working with organisations, Y or N points include: 'Are they Black and minority led?', 'Disability led?', 'Female led?', 'LGBTQ+ led?'; 'Are they affiliated to an Artist Union or an initiative that campaigns for the recognition of artist pay?'; 'How much does this convert into an hourly pay for the duration of the opportunity?'; and 'Can you negotiate this?'

The second page makes you rate the new skills you may or may not acquire, including: 'In your development will it help you be ambitious?' and 'Does it privilege process or outcome?' Plus, most fundamentally: 'Will this give you pleasure?'

This genuinely reflects my thought process when deciding whether to do translation and translation-adjacent work. A big reason

I wanted to become freelance was because I despised having to share an office with a boss who was sexist and homophobic, or another boss who was a bully. I didn't enjoy being around people I found abhorrent, who were also in charge of running and ruining my life. If the financial benefits of writing and translating might always be low, the thing I want to hold on to the most is my ability to have the freedom to decide how I spend my time, and whether I want something in return for it.

Part of my own mental questionnaire includes the following questions:

[ ] Will they ask for the work earlier than the agreed deadline?
[ ] Will my name be on the cover of the book?
[ ] Did they try and haggle my fee?
[ ] Did they offer me more than the minimum rate?
[ ] Will there be a lot of research involved?
[ ] Have I heard of instances of them harassing or bullying translators?
[ ] Is the schedule realistic?
[ ] Am I expected to do a lot of promotion for the book/event?
[ ] Am I in competition with other translators?
[ ] Have I heard good things about the publisher?
[ ] How do they promote translated literature and literary translators?
[ ] Did they get funny about me asking for royalties?
[ ] Are they familiar with my work?

If it frequently doesn't work for you, if it's not fun, why not set your own criteria and stick to them? We *can* rethink the dynamic and remind ourselves that we're freelance so we can have agency. We are the ones being invited to give our time; our time *is* precious. We do have the power to say no in the hope that the time we kept can be used for more worthwhile, more fulfilling things: better work, voluntary work, or just a fun activity with friends during some time off.

I have done work for free or work-swaps for friends and committed to long-term collaborations with others where neither of us is getting paid: but that was my choice.

Pastel blue pie soaring through the air, pink writing in icing coming towards me – *FLUMP!*

Mentoring is bad!

At the above mentoring panel, I was told by a quite established translator that mentoring new translators is bad because there isn't enough work to go around for all of us already in it, and because it gives false hope to emerging translators.

This made me feel very angry. The message here was: translation is full, no room for anyone else. It reminded me of the scepticism, tension and suspicion I experienced when I was trying to get into translating German literature. My intentions were queried, my abilities questioned, my seriousness interrogated. Who are we, as experienced literary translators, to say no? To decide in advance who the best translators might be, who has the potential and who doesn't? What are you afraid of, that someone might be better than you? That you might have to prove yourself? It shows that someone isn't thinking of the art but rather of themselves. Yes, we want to make a living and continue doing this niche job, but it is cruel to shut people out and arrogant to not share skills and welcome others in.

As for false hope, this once more oversteps. A good mentor will be honest about the reality of the vocation, but it is not our place to quash hopes: we're there to fill the mentee with them. Not all mentees want to go into literary translation, they want simply to experience translation. We don't decide who gets to hope and who doesn't. I've been rereading *This Little Art* by Kate Briggs and *A Ghost in the Throat* by Doireann Ní Ghríofa, and both books have this message at their core: anyone should feel like they can have a go at translating literature. We shouldn't take away art schools, literature degrees and writing courses just because not every person will go on to do art or writing as their profession – though the previous government tried their best to do this. Mentors exist to validate and support someone's will to practise an art, and it's up to them to take it as close or as far as they like.

I don't feel afraid when someone says they want to do what I do. I feel excited, energised, relieved that translation is still alive.

Pastel pink pie misses and hits the wall behind me – *BULP!* The shards of pastry and the clumps of cream spell out:

Translating something based on where it will be published is wrong!

At an event I was taking part in on translating poetry, I said that a translator will be influenced by the context in which the translation will be published, meaning that a poem may be translated differently depending on the use for the translation – like being read aloud or appearing in a textbook for language learners – or the publication it was going to appear in – a literary journal versus, perhaps, a cool digital platform aimed at younger people.

Someone in the audience said that they didn't think this was right – and that the poem should simply be translated. A friend of mine also expressed their opinion, quite firmly and forcefully on a separate occasion, that translations should be done without 'messing with the text'.

What I wanted to say both times, but didn't, was this:

Any text or book will be affected by its end destination and perceived intended reader. Even a novel originally written in English will be redrafted and edited differently if set to be published by, say, Prototype, Fitzcarraldo Editions or Faber & Faber; or, if in the process of being read by editorial and marketing departments, it goes from being a book for adults to a book for a young-adult audience; or even if it's a new edition of an old book.

If I were to translate a poem for a textbook for German learners, I probably wouldn't be very creative with my translation because a learner is likely to take the translated words or sentence structure quite literally. Thus, I might hold back on straying too far from the original, even if it sounded somewhat stilted and unidiomatic, or unalive and robotic.

If I were to translate a poem that was only going to be heard at a live reading, I might prioritise how it sounded and aim for greater clarity, so a listener could follow it without needing a second listen or to see the words on the page. If I knew my translation was going to be one of two or three or four or more translations shown together, I might be more adventurous with my translation to accentuate things that others might have downplayed, or to give one very distinctive reading of the piece (which I've actually done before). If I were translating a poem for a cult publication, I might subconsciously or consciously select words within the vocabulary palette of that specific place. Depending on the publication or venue, I might also feel inclined or supported to write a translator's note, footnotes, endnotes, an afterword, an introduction – all additional appendages to the translation, and therefore part of it.

When I did a poetry translation slam where I had to (gently) battle with a fellow translator of the same poem for an audience, the element of my translation that got the most attention and praise was that I had included an English translation of the French epigraph with my translation of the German poem, rather than only keeping the French. I recognised, and knew from experience, that most monolingual English people who hadn't received a prestigious education (and even then...) wouldn't be able to understand the French and would be immediately excluded from the poem at its threshold. Translating the French felt like the fair and friendly thing to do, for me personally, which brings in one of the most important aspects of any translation: it's subjective and will be influenced by the translator's experiences, beliefs, personality, and what feels 'right' for them.

I turn my head as the pastel yellow pie comes at me, it hits me in the ear – *THWUMP!* It whispers:

That word doesn't mean that!

At the same poetry slam, a well-known British poet raised their hand to query my translation. Starting off by saying that they were a mono-lingual English speaker and that they didn't know any German, they had googled one of the words in the original poem – printed in a leaf-let alongside both slamming translations for the audience – and had found that a word I had selected was not the dictionary definition of the word.

Deep breath. My reply was something like the following:

In the original poem, the word had a double meaning because the same word is used for two or more different things in German. My word choice wouldn't match the dictionary definition because I needed a word that held both meanings at once – meanings encased by vastly different words in the English translation that looked and sounded nothing like each other. I had to find a seemingly unrelated English word that could hold shades of both those meanings so the reader of the translation could potentially have a chance at experi-encing the ambiguity and multiplicity created in that moment – a complexity and moment of disorientating joy created by the poet. When making that particular translation decision, I decided to not flatten the word into a single meaning to keep to the most prominent and literal meaning of the word, though another translator could choose to do so, which would also be fine. Translation is a process of choice, a process of prioritising, especially when it comes to translating poetry. Keep rhymes? Keep the same line breaks? Keep metaphors? Keep puns?

The British poet's response? *It doesn't seem right to me; it comes across as a mistake.*

You'd have thought a poet would get this.

A soft chunk of the pastel lilac pie goes straight in my mouth – OMP! I can taste the words:

Only academics should translate literature!

A postgraduate researcher said at an event I was doing with an author I had translated that they thought that only academics should be able to translate literature. They are experts in literature, they're researchers, they understand the socio-historical and socio-political context, they can work on it over many years, was their argument.

When I hear assertions like this, what I hear is that 'only certain people can or should translate books', and then I hear that 'only certain people can or should read books'. Am I not a good enough translator? Am I not a good enough reader?

Writers might be clever and place layers and layers of meaning in their books, but they're not all academics and historians writing to be read by academics and historians. Any astute and focused reader – if the work is doing what it should do, and presuming it isn't seeking a niche or thematically expert reader – should at least be able to pick up on clues and hints that signpost to wider literature. Does a reader need to hold every crumb of knowledge?

Yes, as translators we need to do research, and we do. However, this research can only be expressed creatively, through creative writing, within the parameters set out by a pre-existing work of literature – one that is most likely an acclaimed and supposedly immaculate *tour de force*. What we translate must work as a piece of literature first and foremost. It requires the highest skills in story-telling, story unveiling, knowledge of how to reorchestrate the subtle dynamics and tensions at play, how to maintain a consistent style and voice through every line, paragraph, chapter, the whole novel, so that the book reads as an expertly paced and authentic work of literature, like the original. You have to be a craftsperson, an artist.

Translators are creative-critical maestras: we can write creatively at the highest level and enact deep and multifaceted literary research – often expressed and folded into the lines of the translated text, without a footnote in sight. Academics can most likely do the latter, but not the former. It takes a writer to write a work of literature, translated or otherwise. Writing is not a bonus skill as a translator, it's *the* skill.

I think there's custard in my eye. In my hair. In my mouth.

Apologies for crying and spitting.

Actually, what am I saying?

Can somebody chuck me a towel, I see a queue is forming.

I can take it! Keep the pies coming!

- - - [} - - - [} - - - []

The Translation Game

Your eyes are drawn to flashing coloured lights in the far corner of the Fair.

It's a shiny black retro arcade console with the name *The Translation Game* in gold lettering running across the top. Juddering across the screen are cartoonish caricatures of various literary translators scratching their heads, jumping in the air cheering, peering dejectedly into their wallets, giving a thumbs up.

You put your hand in your pocket and find a golden token.

You push it into the slot.

* E M E R G I N G *

You pull down a big gold handle, and three columns of coloured shapes start scrolling speedily down the screen, before suddenly stopping and revealing your points, which feel like they come directly from your own body:

> You're commissioned to translate the abstracts for an academic conference via someone you met at university (paid) **+1POINT**

Pull again.

> One of the academics commissions you to translate an essay about the sea (paid) **+3POINTS**

Pull again.

> You meet the website editor for a charity at a networking event and they commission you to translate a piece of memoir (unpaid) **+3POINTS**

Pull again.

You're commissioned to translate your first book, a YA story about recycling, after the editor googles 'german translators' and finds your basic new website **+10POINTS**

But! You later find out you got paid half the fee you should have got **–5POINTS**

Pull again.

You think commissions will always come to you, so you wait, but nothing happens for three years **–10POINTS**

Pull again.

You go to a magazine launch and dare to chat to the editor, who has just started a publishing house, about how you want to become a literary translator. They commission you to tranlate a literary work of non-fiction for a proper fee **+20POINTS**

Pull again.

Another publisher notices your name on your translation for the new publisher and contacts you to try out for a novel translation, you get the commission! **+20POINTS**

Pull again.

You self-publish a magazine on German-language culture. A newspaper editor who buys a copy recommends you to their book publisher for a new translation **+20POINTS**

Pull again.

The new publisher recommends you to an established press, which ends up commissioning you **+20POINTS**

Pull again.

The book is shortlisted for a major translation prize
+30 POINTS

Pull again.

No one commissions you for over a year **−60POINTS**

A pixelated Judi Dench appears on screen: 'You're just in someone's eye and then you make something of it and you work again, it's not "good actors" and "bad actors".'

BONUS ROUND!

M U L T I P L E   C H O I C E

A large question mark appears on the screen, overlaid with a box in the shape of a medieval scroll.

Q: A publisher asks you to translate a book for them. An agent told them the book is fantastic, so the publisher bought the rights without having read a word of it. They've only read the publicity material and a sample translation they weren't sure about. You need money to pay the rent, but you're also wary of getting stuck translating something bad.

Do you:

a) Say you'll have to read the book before making a decision;
b) Ask around friends and other translators and read reviews to see if it sounds good;
c) Agree to do the job.

What will you choose?

You selected a: The publisher couldn't wait, so they've already asked someone else who can start work straight away! It turns out the book is brilliant/terrible!

You selected b: The book isn't out yet so there aren't any reviews; one friend says they loved it, one says they hated it! You still have no idea and opt to/not/take it on. It turns out to be brilliant/terrible!

You selected c: You're anxious for the whole first draft and it turns out to be incredibly hard/incredibly boring/incredibly offensive/incredible.

Would you like to continue playing?

Cats and Pigs

Yes, you may stroke the cats. They're everywhere, I know, wandering around, sleeping in the stands, begging for gnawed-down chicken bones. I think they're here because in Malta there are hundreds and hundreds of stray cats; you pull open a mewing bush and you'll see a dozen kittens. There are cat homes in the villages for them to sleep in. You can also stroke the pigs; they chew the unstoppable weeds that sprout through the gaps in the linoleum floor tiles. I have always been fixated on how a line from a book I translated came out as 'small black pig', it just seemed like a perfect trio of words, I like saying it over and over again. Small black pig. Small black pig. My mum even knitted me a small black pig, it's perfect and has wonky ears. My reading Frank Wynne's translation of *Règne animal – Animalia* – by Jean-Baptiste Del Amo – a multigenerational novel about pig farming and animal/ human cruelty – coincided with P. Staff's exhibition 'On Venus' at the Serpentine Gallery, which included videos of lambs being abused. This combo meal finally made me vegetarian. A goat is like a cat, a pig is like a cat, they're the same but different, it's a matter of perception.

A hangover in German is a Kater, which literally means 'tomcat' but actually means hangover. How would I translate it? Just as 'hangover'? Or the poetic 'a tomcat of a hangover' to keep the effect, the virile and aggressive undertone, that other layer of meaning?

The cats love chewing the weeds and plants we have around the place. One of the plants is Pistaziengrün – literally 'pistachio green', but in English it's a foliage that can be called pistache or lentisque, or other things. Would we say 'she could smell the pistache' or 'she smelled the pistachio green of the lentisque', keeping that nice flash of colour – I do love colour – and creating a lovely chime between 'pis' and 'tis' (a bell chimes)? Is that too far, perhaps turning a molehill into a mole mound? (We have moles here too.)

In Kuba Szreder's book *The ABC of the Projectariat*, which is about art workers but could be about literary translators, H is for Herding Cats:

63

The projectarians are a curious bunch. On the one hand, they are social animals, constantly in touch with other people. On the other hand, they are lone wolves, in that they are one-person business ventures. [...] Anyone who has tried to organize a union of art workers, pull off an art strike or maintain a long-term struggle knows very well that these feats are as difficult as herding cats. On the other hand, a black cat is a symbol of wildcat strikes, often adopted by the anarchist trade unions and collectives to underline their untamed yet ferocious character.

Szreder translated his own book from Polish into English, his examples are drawn from the pushback against poor working conditions for artists, predominantly women.

Because I know German, I have been reading and following the pushback against bad pay, working conditions and AI (translation: faulty and unethical plagiarism software) by literary translators in the German context. While here in the UK we're still like independent cats, they have gathered and formed large collectives and made a big impact. I want to translate what they've done so more people can access it. The translation of socio-political events can inspire, spread energy, show that we're not alone in our struggle. One German translator wrote an essay for a major German-language newspaper; she could have been writing about my experience. There were hundreds of comments telling her to stop whining, to quit, that she was greedy like a pig.

Telegraph

Standing tall among the stands are telegraph poles with drooping wires hanging between them. They connect up the stands so that they can communicate with one another.

When my dad came over to England from Malta, he worked in a frozen food warehouse and then was a bus driver for twelve years, fixing up cars in his spare time. He left school when he was eight and worked as a mechanic throughout the rest of his childhood and teenagerhood. When my mum got pregnant with me, he got a job as an engineer at British Telecom. He would have to go up telegraph poles in the middle of the night, sometimes in horrendous storms, and dig up roads to fix wiring, to keep lines of communication open.

He has always worked extremely hard, and though modest, has always sought credit for the work he has done. He tells a story about a manager of his who tried to pass off a PowerPoint presentation as his own at a meeting, only to realise my dad had password-protected it just as the presentation was about to begin. And another time someone had stolen his plans for a specific kind of wire casing, not knowing that my dad had encoded his name in the footer of the document. Gloriously petty. Or simply glorious. I did a couple of Take Your Daughter to Work Days when he was at BT, and at one of them I had to construct a wire casing from instructions, then dip it in a bucket to see if the casing I'd put together was watertight, that it would keep the lines of communication open. My mum's family wouldn't talk to him for a long time, even after they were married, because he was a foreigner, only opening up channels again when I was born.

You wouldn't have been able to tell that my dad is Maltese and that my mum was half Irish from our house growing up – no photos, no cultural artefacts. It was a void of family and cultural history.

I understand now that there were reasons for that.

The only time I would hear my dad speak Maltese was when he was on the phone to my granddad or uncle. I couldn't help but stand near him in the kitchen when he was on the phone. I would discern that his opening words, Orrajt, ħi? Kollox sew?, meant Alright, dear? How are you?, but then the rest would be a secret. I think I went into languages because I wanted to have my own secret. When I told my family that I wanted to keep studying languages, my dad, who hadn't taught us his own language, Maltese, said that German was a 'real language'. My Maltese is trapped in a phoneline somewhere, heading somewhere else.

Hot Chocolate Stand

The first thing I ever ordered in a German café was a hot chocolate.

Ich möchte eine heiße Schokolade... mit Sahne.
I would like a hot chocolate... with cream.

I hadn't yet progressed from the taught, stock, stiff Ich möchte (I would like) to the more typical, casual Ich hätte gerne (I'd like/I'll have). This was also the first time I had been to a café on my own. It was a day off from au pairing, and I didn't have any friends yet in Munich. I could pick anything I wanted. I was eighteen, I didn't yet drink tea or coffee, and it was a freezing cold day. I think I chose hot chocolate because I had always liked the way it felt to say *high-sssser shocko-laaader*. I'd had hot chocolate when I was in the Scouts that was like brown boiling water that smelled chocolatey but tasted of nothing, or as a treat I'd have a flavoured powdered chocolate sachet at home. This was the most amazing hot chocolate, made so luxurious with the thickest, creamiest cream.

I'm always intrigued to read about the childhoods of infamous translators, often ones of travel and parents with prestigious jobs. Maureen Freely's father moves the family to Turkey when he's lecturing there, and she eavesdrops on his students. Lydia Davis speaks of spending some of her childhood in Austria, her parents both writers for the *New Yorker*, having hot chocolate for breakfast. For breakfast!

When I read these accounts, I fantasise about what it would have been like to have had experiences in a foreign country earlier on, as a child, open to the world, rather than late in my teenage years, at my most closed off and insecure. I'm intrigued by their multilingual upbringings as much as I am by their experiences of private schools, these foreign-seeming places with their own lingo. Imagination inserts me in their stories.

Today I read an online post made by a cultural institution regarding a book by one of the authors I translated. It simply says: *The book has also been translated into English.*

It's passive and mysterious, it's matter of fact, like it got dipped in chocolate.

A magazine in America is holding an event for one of my translations. The invite reads: *To celebrate the release of an English edition.*

Like a brand announcing a new flavour of hot choc.

Beware: Prickly Pear

When I was working that job as a tour guide at an art fair, there were huge *Monstera deliciosa* (Swiss cheese plants) placed around the fair in enormous pots. They felt like a reminder of the outside that we wouldn't see all day, or a way to give the place a sense of naturalness, an organic wilderness.

Here, in the fair, *Opuntia*, or prickly pear cactuses – indigenous to Malta – grow out of the cracks in the walls, the splits in the floor, hang from the rafters.

Sometimes your clothes snag on them, or you back into them.

Sometimes you get the minuscule but agonising spines in your lips and tongue where they've fallen into your food.

X7 – Workshop Room 1: Salt Dough Workshop

Come make some fake food with me!

Here are a few items on plinths from the recreation at Thaddaeus Ropac Gallery of an iconic Sturtevant exhibition in which she recreated replica food objects by Claes Oldenburg. There's a papier-mâché frying pan holding a papier-mâché fried egg, a papier-mâché scoop of vanilla ice cream in a shallow glass goblet, a papier-mâché burger. They look like the originals, but they're slightly different.

We can edit writing, including translations, in a workshop, and yet there are no tools and there is little mess. 'Workshop' sounds very physical and hands on and industrious and productive – in a way they are physical, they are hands on, attendees are industrious and productive. The effort that goes in is mental, but marks are made, bodies move. Still, the word feels co-opted, appropriative somehow.

I think of times when someone asks what I'm doing when I'm reading something and I respond, I'm working. I get my dad's voice teasing me in my head, *Doesn't look like work to me.*

Since I was a child I've wanted to be a writer, but the older I get the more ashamed I become that I can't do anything with my hands. Using a computer or a notebook and pen all day to write and translate needs the body, fingers to type, back to sit, eyes to wince and droop at a screen. I mutter and talk to myself. I make my eyes roll from side to side or in an arc when I'm tracking an idea. If you ask me what I do, I'll say it's akin to remaking something or weaving, I'll say that I unpick sentences and rethread them, I untangle them like ropes, wires, nets. I embroider, I layer up paint and scrape it off. I weld. I smash apart and reassemble from the fragments. This is all metaphorical. I'm just a person whose wrists ache, and who produces no physical trace of my effort – someone else makes my marks into a book-object.

I've recently become covetous of jobs that have overalls and aprons, costumes that denote graft. Richard commissioned a maker friend of ours, Lucy, to make me a tabard – a navy apron with deep mint-green pockets – which I wear when I translate. I'm a bit of an anomaly among our friends – many of them are painters, sculptors, illustrators, potters, set designers, people who don't balk at the prospect of building shelves, making a pair of trousers, handmaking decorations for a wedding reception, as Lucy did for our wedding.

When I put the translation tabard on, I feel like I'm going to work, that I'm going to be doing something active that requires energy and transformation. When I stand in the kitchen and drink a cup of tea, I think of my dad taking a break from fixing a car, sitting on the back step smeared with oil, drinking scalding Nescafé.

When I take off the tabard, the working day is done – I have sustained a period of working, set by the clock of the uniform, as opposed to hours of 'playing' at working in my everyday clothes. But no matter how much I can trick myself into thinking I'm a maker, I'm not wearing an apron to protect me from spatter and spillage. The mess remains in my mind, I carry around the clutter and half-made things wherever I go. The working day is never truly over.

I was scrolling through the Internet while being cradled in the distracting, comforting void of my phone during the early stage of the pandemic, when I saw a group of four photos displaying the work of the American sculptor Claes Oldenburg, whose work I wasn't previously familiar with.

There was a glass counter like one you might find in a supermarket or a canteen with what looked like large slices of bread slathered with various spreads, though you could tell that they were fake by their uniformity, and from the fact that though some of the toppings could have been chocolate or mayonnaise, others were bright orange or yellow – it was actually thickly applied paint. Then there were pieces that, though more abstract, could easily be interpreted as two hamburgers – gooey and melting, with thick layers of paint designating a hamburger's distinctive rainbow. Finally, there were two dessert display cases like you get in American diners or Italian restaurants, with brightly coloured blobs in silver dishes (ice cream) and chunky triangles on ceramic plates (slices of pie).

I was mesmerised by them, their subdued and pastel colours, their misshapen, childish quality, how fun they were, how happy they made me feel, and though I hadn't made anything in my whole life, I became fixated with wanting to try and replicate them in my own small way.

I showed Richard the photos as he's an artist himself, and he said they reminded him of a young artist who makes replica beer cans and tinned food and other everyday items out of a cheap material called salt dough. All I would need is salt and flour, and we had a little of both of these. That night I sat up in bed doodling (when was the last time I doodled?) a page, then another page, of things I would like to make. A doughnut, a baguette, a croissant, a slice of pizza, a slice of watermelon, a diamond ring. A tube of toothpaste, rolled up and squeezed. A banana, a bulb of garlic, a set of salt and pepper shakers, a cup of coffee, a fried egg, and, of course, a piece of toast spread with jam. My mind filled with whimsical, mainly edible objects.

The next day, a Saturday, I mixed together the basic ingredients – one cup of plain flour, half a cup of salt, half a cup of lukewarm water – briefly kneaded, and began forming my models. A doughnut. A hot cross bun and a Belgian bun. A pretzel and a slice of toast. A toothpaste tube and an independent, wiggling streak of toothpaste. Half a sandwich.

I floured my hands and the rolling pin. I had a little dish of water to use to glue pieces together and to smooth out the drying, cracking surfaces. I only looked at my phone for reference images. I baked them in the oven on the lowest setting for two and a half hours, and I felt guilty and foolish when I smelled that baked-goods smell in the knowledge that I was making something inedible and un-nourishing with precious flour. When they came out, slightly puffed up and a little browned, I actually felt proud and at ease for the first time in months. I remember that I'm not the only translator with a making impulse, not even for small things: <u>Julia Sanches</u> and <u>Marta Dziurosz</u> make ceramics, <u>Bruna Dantas Lobato</u> makes miniatures.

On the Sunday, I put on an apron (one I used to wear when I worked Friday and Saturday evening shifts at a supermarket on the cheese and meat counter and would need to drain and clean the chicken rotisserie oven with choking chemicals) and laid out some acrylic paints. I began carefully painting these objects. Why did I want to make these silly, twee, kitschy things? I tried to rationalise and intellectualise it. They were translations of my appreciation of Oldenburg! They were a comment on the impulse for consumerism as a form of comfort during crisis! They're proof that cultural icons are a form of iconic language! But they were ultimately useless models.

I had a lot of work I could be doing or getting involved with. I'd followed a collective of translators, some of whom I know and greatly admire, going into overdrive to translate a collectively written novel about lockdown by Portuguese-language authors. I had translations to be working on, but I couldn't face them.

Many years ago, I tried to involve my dad in a translation workshop, pretty much against his will. Out of a wish to bond over something I cared about – literary translation – I suggested we translate a poem from Maltese together. I'm a writer and translator, he knows Maltese, it should work, I reasoned. It failed. Why? 'It's nonsense,' he said. Though he could read Maltese, he had never read a poem in his life. So: I couldn't read the Maltese, he couldn't decipher the poetry, neither of us could read or translate the poem.

After a lifetime of disconnect between my dad and me due to our clash of interests and professions, we'd finally found a meeting ground. I sent him pictures of my salt dough models and he liked them, he was impressed, perhaps the most impressed he's ever been with something I've done. I don't mean that he isn't proud of my achievements, but they're abstract to both of us – everyone can appreciate a nicely made model fried egg.

I had an idea, but I was nervous to ask him. When replying to an email about the models, I asked my dad if he wanted to make some with me over Skype. He said he would like to, he couldn't wait! We'd not made anything together since school transitioned from doing and making into writing and studying. I decide to make an English breakfast; he wants to make replica mechanic's tools.

Joining a Skype call together where we'd be showing one another what we'd made and what we were struggling with, and the creative decisions we were making, made me think of the emerging translator mentoring I'd been doing for the last couple of years, and every other morning for the last few weeks, where I'd helped people of all ages, all over the world, think about approaches to translating and editing and pitching online. This was a new dynamic for us, I was the more experienced one, and he listened to my advice.

We stayed on this call for two hours, as opposed to the usual fifteen to thirty minutes. I think this is because we had portions of time where neither of us said much, and because the making together was a kind of talking together in a language we both understood, or a kind of bilingualism, an instance of translanguaging (a word I wouldn't use with my dad) where there's what's being said and the subtext being pummelled into dough or directed into the slit caused by a knife.

I may not be able to speak Maltese, his language, but I now understand this is a way of communicating I hadn't considered and perhaps one he would prefer; that simply being together and producing something together is a kind of talking. It's poetic without even mentioning poetry, it's close via the vulnerability of making something in front of each other.

The food is fake, not the real thing, but what is real is that an actual person worked to make it, and they had a real experience.

X8 – Workshop Room 2: Anti-Sexual Harassment Workshop

All visible staff on site have been specially trained in how to respond to sexual harassment.

The training undertaken is one of two different kinds of workshops I led within the D.I.Y. punk scene that gave me the confidence to teach literary translation.

When I was a senior trainer at a grassroots anti-sexual harassment organisation, founded by someone I knew in D.I.Y. punk, Bryony Beynon, I would lead workshops to train staff in night-time venues how to respond to reports of sexual harassment or assault.

It was an at times challenging but wholly rewarding experience. It taught me a method of teaching where a person in a workshop is listened to, validated, offered a new way of seeing something, and then given the chance to ask any follow up questions before the session moves on.

Sometimes people would hold very strong and at times abhorrent views that I would then have to try and walk them through while remaining open and calm.

One of the tasks was to offer up a variety of myths around sexual assault:

Women lie for attention.
It is always someone of a certain race who commits assault.
There is serious and less serious sexual violence.

I adapted this task to my translation workshops:

You always need to have a degree in a language to become a translator.
Editors have the right to change your translation in total or in part.
Every translator is entitled to translate any text.

When I would give press interviews, it was repeatedly put to me that this opt-in training for venues (venues don't legally need training) was political correctness gone mad and that it was patronising. Would someone say that about fire safety?, I would counter. Training people in how to handle sexual harassment and assault isn't sanitising a space and sucking the fun out of it – it's just good health and safety.

Not repeating stereotypes or sexist, racist, ableist, homophobic, transphobic language in a translation when it's not justifiable (when it's not, for instance, something said by a character with discriminatory views, or in a sarcastic tone or satirical mode, or when the writer is repeating experiences verbatim – and even these can be up for discussion depending on context and intended audience) isn't censorship – it's just mindful, responsive editing.

Even when translating my very first book, a non-fiction book for young people, I knew that it was bad writing when the author depicted a man seeking refuge using racist stereotypes and myths, and even though I knew nothing about what happens when translations are edited, I flagged it with the editor and said it shouldn't be in the translation. They agreed.

When we talk about women's safety, it's health and safety; when we talk about activist translation, we're really talking about good translation.

X9 – Workshop Room 3: Drumming Workshop

Everyone pick up a pair of sticks, a pair of ear defenders, and sit down at one of these shiny purple drumkits.

While living in Munich, I went to gigs two or three times a week at a small club. I would always fixate on the drummers, and would ask for a signed drumstick after shows. I had quite a collection at one point, a dozen or more.

Let's quickly run over to the room of beds, the bed from my WG.

I used to sit on the edge of the bed holding a pair of mismatched drumsticks, and would use my thighs as a snare, practise drum rolls on my pillow. I sought out a drumming teacher and crossed the city a few times to go down into this guy's basement, where he mainly got me to watch him drum. Once, on one of the rare times he let me sit at the kit, he said that women lacked the physical strength to drum properly. I stopped going to the lessons, continued to play in my room on my bed and body, and learnt how to drum by playing in bands at university, by playing with others.

At our local DIY punk venue in London, my friend Tamsin and I once gave a drumming workshop for women and non-binary wannabe drummers as part of the festival You Can't Be What You Can't See, created by fellow musician, Bryony, who also founded the organisation that provides anti-harassment workshops.

I was very nervous about giving the workshop. I wasn't a drumming teacher or a professional musician, I had no formal qualifications in drumming, I had just played drums in bands for a decade. On the days we gave the workshops I was shocked to realise how much I knew about drumming. About the equipment, about the dynamics with the rest of the band during practice and performing, the tricks of the trade and the things you don't really need to worry about.

If I could teach drumming, I thought, if I could teach anti-harassment procedures, I reasoned, I could teach literary translation; I knew things I could pass on. The point of the drumming workshops was to encourage and empower those still excluded from music and certain instruments. I wanted to do this with literary translation, so I organised a few free mentorships for those from backgrounds traditionally excluded from literary translation and publishing. The other workshops had got me to this point.

X10 – Workshop 4: Knitting Workshop

Everyone pick up a pair of needles and a ball of wool, we have every colour, every texture. Knit if you can knit, help each other out. Alternatively, you can be a detangler and pull apart knotted clumps of wool. Or drum on your legs with the blunt ends.

Working from home has always made sense to me. My mum was only able to work for a couple of years in her early twenties and then had to stop due to mental illness, so would read, knit, watch TV at home. My best friend and her family lived next door, and her mum was (and still is) a full-time sculptor who worked out in her studio in the garden, but also invariably in the house.

My mum and her mum made me feel that art and craft can be done at home. My friend took after her mother and makes sculptures at home; I took after mine by staying at home and taking in/making art. (I sometimes wish I could put a piece of plastic sheeting over my computer and the book I'm translating to stop them drying out and cracking.)

My mum was once renowned for her knitting. At one point she sold bobble hats on eBay, but then turning her hobby/passion into a business got too much, the pressure to produce started to take the enjoyment out of it.

If you look on the walls you can see patchwork woollen blankets my mum knitted over the years. This one straight ahead, with squares in different shades of purple and lilac, is usually on my bed. My mum's blankets are precious because I can tell she made them, they have the odd dropped stitch yet they still keep me warm.

X11 – Workshop 5: Translation Workshop/Easter Eggs

Come in, sit down in groups at the tables, there are hot drinks available. Hot chocolate, Nescafé.

Here's an *almost* 'literal' not-translation/record of the opening of Gregor Hens's book *Nikotin*, or *Nicotine*. This is a combination of the flicker of the moment of reading-in-German and comprehension-in-English that happens in my mind and which never reaches a document, and the real multiple options a word throws up in the dictionary, as well as those I place in the first draft of my actual translation as there is often not a single equivalent, partly because English is a larger language with more options, each with something unique – a nuance, a rhythm, a sound, how it might fit nicely with other words in the sentence. This is just one/my version of an artificial not-literal not-translation; another translator might do it differently, so please don't go thinking it's *a* or *the* literal translation.

I've created this hodgepodge for you as a jumping-off point, so you can get into my mind and into my first draft, and so you can get the experience of translating. Why not try and make this text into something closer to an English text? What words will you use? Will you insert the detail about why bacon rind is used? Will you adapt the lines? Will the voice sound how you sound?

Nikotin – pre-translated by Jen

There are men/humans/people, by which/with whom I like/gladly/willingly a cigarette smoke would – friends, who/which I long not seen have, artists, who/which I venerate/admire/marvel-at. The most of them smoke not more. Several/some are already dead. With my grandfather, in whose vast/huge/enormous, horny/calloused hand the cigarette always so thin/skinny and fragile/frail/brittle appeared/looked, would-have I like/gladly/willingly a/one-of smoked. He is too early died. I am positive/convinced, that he died is, because one from-him in/inside the hospital, in which he after a overthrow/fall delivered/admitted was, the cigarettes away-taken had. Although/even though he only five to ten on-a day smoked had, sixty years long. My grandfather was a greatly/exceedingly/overly restrained/modest man/person. If/when he whole mornings in his kitchen sat and on a out-spread/unfolded newspaper lentils sorted, potatoes skinned/peeled or with a bacon-rind Easter-eggs polished/buffed*, lay the box/packet with the slipped-in match-book always it-beside, like/how a promise.

I have often this-of dreamt, one-time in an art-historical museum to smoke. I have myself imagined, I would me on a/one-of this/these slick/smooth/sleek, by the skewed/oblique/slanting/slantwise/obliquely invading/incoming afternoon-sun warmed massive/sturdy wood-bench sit, and me a cigarette stick/torch/up-light, a filter-less cigarette, which unfortunately since some years from-the market vanished/missing/disappeared is. I have no doubt, that this a moment of-absolute lucidity/clarity/serenity for me would-be, perhaps my all-greatest fortune/luck/happiness. It will not this-to come. I smoke not/no more/longer.

* Dyed eggs are rubbed with bacon fat to stop them from going bad

....
....
....
....
....

This is still a bit of a trick. Only I can read the tone, only I can hear his voice.

Easter Egg Hunt

Take a basket!

There are Easter eggs in the text, things you don't always explain or translate. Street names. References. You need to know references are references in order for the reference to possibly survive. There are no guarantees, like my Tamagotchi that I fed and cared for, but then a stream of Japanese would appear to announce that it had died nonetheless.

I need to know that something is a reference so that I can lay the clues for this reference in my translation – if I know it's a reference, like a quote, I have to make sure the quote is recognisable to someone who would know it. Some people won't get the reference anyway, and my job isn't to make the reference even more remarkable – but I have to put down the clues so it will be possible to those who can clock it.

It's often incredibly hard to figure out if something is a reference. There were many references in Marion Poschmann's *The Pine Islands*; sometimes sentences 'felt' like they were referential and I would go hunting online, other times something seemed like a non sequitur. I felt pride in finding what I thought was an obscure reference and proudly showed it to Marion, a dozen eggs in my hands, to which she replied that it wasn't actually a reference at all, but that she really liked the quote I'd found and wanted it kept in.

Ultimately, you can't expect your author to point out every reference in the book; they might not even remember, or it might open a wormhole of intertextuality we don't want to try and deal with. It slides into the notion that 'translation is impossible'. And that's not even looking at how German is not English — the German language and the English language, despite their shared origins and resulting similarities, still have very separate histories and etymologies and can't be non-referential and non-intertextual; they've lived unique lives, including in their literatures. (There's an episode of *Star Trek* where Captain Jean-Luc Picard learns an alien language that is all metaphors based on myths and legends in the alien culture. This is a spectacular, heightened version of how idioms within languages come from shared knowledge, but also languages in general – you have to ignore the fact that the alien language isn't that alien, as it's still English.)

One author kept her Easter egg to herself – I only found out about an important secret theme running through the book in an interview the author gave a year after my translation came out. She might have forgotten, she might have buried the memory, though she did say that she thought most of the references in the book were 'obvious'. Though it didn't affect the book as a whole, I would have loved to have made choices that nodded and hinted towards this hidden thing that only certain readers would have picked up on.

One author I had to ask over and over again whether things were references to something, as I didn't understand them. They said they were things they'd seen in their dreams.

When translating Helene Bukowski, I found two ambiguities that were not supposed to be ambiguities. Lines that, when tapped and cracked open, spilled multiple yolks of possibility, rather than one. Helene changed the original text when it had a reprint because of the bad/abundant eggs I'd found.

Basement – Puppet Show

Take a lantern when you exit the lift, it's dark in the woods in the basement, but not for long. There's a clearing ahead, you can see the glow in the distance. That's it, slip down the slope or take the newly installed wheelchair ramp to your left.

What you see in front of you aren't apparitions but fourteen television screens, a few partially submerged in the forest floor, or in a pile of leaves, or sunken into the trunk of a tree.

The only constant chatting we had in our house was from the televisions of which my dad had bought a job lot, and which we had in every room. Our parents didn't read to us and we didn't have many books, so we watched a lot of TV.

I learnt my ABCs from *Sesame Street*, which is why I say 'zee' and not 'zed', 'haitch' and not 'aitch'.

The screen eventually extended to the page. The screen or the page is like a two-way mirror, where I can watch without being watched. All my barriers are down, and I can absorb and learn from what I see without the worry of having to give anything back, even a facial expression. I still find it hard to emote.

On each screen is a looped episode of *The StoryTeller*, a Jim Henson-produced, Anthony Minghella-scribed television series I watched as a child that featured retellings of old fairy tales – 'some of the most adventurous and inventive variations on the material ever made for television', according to Marina Warner – told by a mix of actors, actors in animatronic costumes, and terrifying puppets. There's 'Sapsorrow', a take on 'Cinderella', 'Fearnot', also known as 'The Boy Who Went Out to Learn How to Shudder', 'Hans My Hedgehog', 'The Three Ravens', 'The Luck Child', 'The Soldier and Death' and more. They're synced to all start playing the theme music simultaneously. A stabbing cello joined by a breathy flute with a crow cawing over it – it still gives me the heebie-jeebies.

John Hurt, who played the storyteller himself, speaks over the music in an echoey voice, listen!

When people told themselves their past with stories, explained their present with stories, foretold their future with stories, the best place by the fire was kept for the storyteller.

While the final dregs of a clarinet toot off, there is a surtitle over a fire that says something like, 'From a traditional German folktale' or 'a Russian fable', before Hurt's face appears, knobbly with cheek and nose prosthetics, and he begins his distinctive way of weaving these old yarns, full of 'dearies' (referring to the viewers, or his talking dog) and his ominous, low-registered 'oh dearrr, oh dearrr' to warn of impending doom.

Stories used to roam free and ride in storytellers' minds, worn smooth like a well-sucked lozenge in a mouth. Sometimes they tweak the recipe for the story soup.

Rebecca Solnit read fairy tales online for her nieces and nephews and the rest of the world during the Covid lockdown and made little alterations – the Little Mermaid returns to her sisters, for instance, and she's previously retold 'Cinderella', where everyone, including the evil sisters and the stepmother, is freed from their roles.

But now, my dears, stories are set in stone. We no longer need storytellers to pass on stories, they're transported by print. The old stories multiplied and became furnished with new details, and we can no longer see the connection with the old stories.

It was the way John Hurt told the stories that made them for me, the rhythm of his voice, his presence, which ran like a thread through all these fairy tales. More and more often, famous writers are asked to adapt old foreign-language stories: Solnit, for instance.

I wish translators of literature were viewed as storytellers. People seem wary of the idea, but translators don't even alter the stories they tell, they try their best to keep every detail.

I think it's because people think to themselves: 'Who is this nobody telling me a story?'

In the making-of documentary for the new Netflix remake of another of my childhood favourites, Jim Henson's *The Dark Crystal*, one of the puppeteers says something that could be about being a literary translator:

> I don't think puppeteers are well known, by the nature of their job they are hidden. There's [sic] very few famous puppeteers, it is an art where you choose to hide. And I very much think it's like a musician, that you have an instrument and you play a beautiful tune on it and it's the tune we remember, it's not necessarily the piano it was played on.

I'd say that the piano isn't the puppeteer, the piano is language, and a piano is as inert as a wooden puppet without someone to move it. Translators are like ventriloquists, but we're also the ventriloquist's dummy. We do the voices but are also the wooden proxy for the author, who controls our every move.

Can you tell it's our voice every time? A voice I find comforting is Brian Henson's. He did the voice for the goblin Hoggle in *Labyrinth*, the dog in *The StoryTeller*, Jack Pumpkinhead in the equally puppet-led *Return to Oz*. His voice is so distinctive, but changes subtly every time. It has its own particular qualities.

Elsewhere in the documentary, the actor Simon Pegg could also be talking about translation; he even unknowingly critiques the well-known metaphor that reading a translation is like looking through a pane of glass for making the process too invisible:

> The point with puppetry is it's a medium, it's an art form in itself, and that's what you're watching, it helps you stay slightly detached and think about it a bit more, you don't just get hypnotised by it, looking through a window, you know, you're looking at something which is a representation.

He also says:

> In the original film, not that it mattered and not that I cared
> and not that it was ever a thing, but you can occasionally see
> a rod now and again, you know, not that that means 'Oh, wait
> a minute, there's a rod! It's not real!' Course it's not real, it's a
> puppet show, you should be able to see all the rods really.

Actor Taron Egerton sums it up nicely, and he too could be talking
about literary translation:

> You're indulging in an illusion. [...] Through a collection of
> great performers and great makers, the audience are able to
> invest in this thing and believe that it's real life, and there's
> something really magical about that.

If you go straight ahead you'll come to my workshop, where I've been
making alterations. Come in and warm up, I have a fire going. You
can sit there, by the workbench.

Up on that shelf are the quality glues, hanging from those hooks
are the sharpened scissors, and the top-end printer is underneath in
an alcove to your left.

I've been inserting translators in copies of their translations on the
sly and planting them in bookshops. 'From a contemporary German
novel' or 'From a modern Turkish book of short stories' is now on
the title page. The moment you see and hear them introduce the
story, you know that everything that comes after is a retelling.

Here's a batch I've been working on for <u>Emily Wilson</u>. Here's a photo
of her reading her translation of the *Odyssey* to her three daughters
and three cats, and they're all dressed up as characters from the epic.

I've carefully pasted it into copies of the book alongside a photo
of her giving a reading from it in New York, with her arms raised and
accompanied by shadow puppets on the wall behind her, and a photo
of her in a school production of the *Odyssey* as a young girl. There are

a few words from her about what the book means to her, addressing the reader in a familiar way, gleaned in part from what she's said in interviews, she's very busy.

It's the first translation into English by a woman and is unblighted by the misogyny of some of her male predecessors' attempts. All storytellers have power, be they writers, tellers or translators.

I like the way Rebecca Solnit tells the stories of others, the rhythm of her voice, her presence, which runs through all her essays.

I like the way certain translators tell the stories of others, the rhythm of their voices, their presence, which runs through their translations.

I wonder if I will see all my childhood favourites remade, and I wonder who'll do all the remaking? Can you give me a hand piling up these messed-with *Odysseys*?

The clever title of Jenn Shapland's memoir-cum-biography of Carson McCullers, *My Autobiography of Carson McCullers*, gets close to the strangeness of the fact that a translation is something that is the translator's, and also not the translator's.

Michael Gambon, who played the eponymous storyteller in the Greek Myths series of *The StoryTeller* (the storyteller is both John Hurt and Michael Gambon), quoted by Tom Hollander: 'They've asked me to play a twelfth-century German-speaking one-legged pope. You know what? Turns out he's just like me.' 'I'm going to be playing a Mongolian shepherd who dreams of being a trapeze artist. You know what...?' A character emanates from a writer, a character emanates from the writer via a translator.

What could we put on the front of the book?

Emily Wilson wrote/didn't write the Odyssey
Emily Wilson's Homer's Odyssey

One day I'd like to start Jen Calleja's Workshop – like Jim Henson's Workshop or an artists' studio with a troupe of assistants, where everyone learns my way of translating and spends their time work-shopping translations in my style.

I can have an overview and let everyone else do the work. Maybe.

What's important to know is that words are just words until someone comes along to bring them to life: 'A puppet is just a bag of glue and fur,' the puppeteer Eric says in the series *Eric*, 'until someone sticks its hand up its ass. My hand!'

T3 – Non-Translator Translation Roundtable

with:

Rebecca Frecknall (my best friend at university), theatre director

Elaine Lillian Joseph (a new friend and possible future mentor), audio describer

Sam Brewster (my former studio mate), illustrator and filmmaker

Francesca Wade (former editor of *The White Review*, where one of my translations was published), biographer

What do a theatre director, an audio describer, a biographer and an illustrator have to do with translation? Their roles require interpretation, the recreation of an original in a new form, and they've seen their piecemeal pay stagnate. Hear what they each think about the state of their translatory practices. Francesca, would you like to start?

Francesca Wade: 'Most reviews of biographies assess the life rather than the book. So often [...] biographers (rather like translators) get praised for being as unobtrusive as possible – as if every sentence, every interpretation, wasn't a choice they made!'

Oh, sorry, we'll have to leave it there as everyone has work to do.

POSTPONED DUE TO LACK OF AVAILIBILITY

Carousel

Hop on the carousel, or merry-go-round. I can't translate for an odd hour here or there; if I sit down to translate, it might be six hours, nine hours, longer. I need to reach a flow state, let the text put up the railings and set the course. I used to write on buses and translate on trains and planes, a real movement added to the readerly journey, but then I started feeling nauseous. If I can't get in the flow, I can't do it, simple as that. I can try and force it, but I get distracted with looking up words, or what I write sounds too German. Translator's block.

A publisher asks if I can translate a sample of a short story collection: 'How fast can you do it?' Do people expect writers to write stories as fast as possible? Or artists to paint as quickly as possible? Why is speed the greatest factor? I'm not sitting around and waiting for work, I'm already on the carousel. Faster, faster, faster, faster!!!

G78 – Urchin and Leech

On the floor of the stand is an installation of spiky urchins and slippery leeches, both black like inkblots on the white floor.

On the back wall is a projection of a video of Michelle Steinbeck and I giving a reading together in the basement of the Poetry Café in London.

She held her laptop up for the course of the reading while I stood next to her, and we each read translations of each other's poetry before we read texts about what it was like meeting each other for the first time and spending a week together when I joined her on her residency in Rome.

I had written mine in English, and she had written hers in German before live-translating it.

Here she is, unfazed at having to translate her text before a full room.

I am very excited for Jen. I get her at the train station. I hope we will find each other, and find each other nice. I say: we go out for dinner. Do you eat everything? Everything, she says. We go to the Bacala Fritta. Jen finds it *delish*. She asks me a lot of questions, and I answer loudly and in too much detail. We drink wine. We run through the Death Tunnel [*a very loud tunnel for road traffic and not intended for authors and translators*, I whisper as an aside to whoever is closest to me] and Jen's afraid. I scream *woooo!* in the noisy din, and *it's like a dream!* I've been wrong two times. Jen is no vegan and she's not chain-smoking either. Jen tells me how she found my book. In the German cultural centre there it was, she saw the cover and asked the Librarian, *do you know that?* She said, *Ja, it's the strangest thing I've ever read.* Then we go eat. We take pasta. I take it with ricci [*that's sea urchins*, I shout to all of you over the sound of the video], which the woman at the next table had just complained about because there was nothing on it. She behaves terribly. Jen tells me how as a teenager she worked on a meat counter in a supermarket and somebody said *I want ten slices of ham, if you can count that high*, and she put her apron down and left. The … Kellner? [I lean in and whisper to Michelle: *waiter*] … *waiter* is dismayed because of the woman. And as I say that I want what she didn't want he asks me if I know it and if I am sure and everything three times and I say *yeah yeah yeah bring it to me*. The food comes and Jen says *I've never eaten anything like this before, but it's delish*. The pasta comes and mine smells fish. There's really not much on it. A bit of parsley on the side and on top two blob clots. I put them on the side and eat the spaghetti. I have to eat it because I bragged so much about it to the waiter. We drink the wine and Jen tells me about how she once had a spinal tap and I think, *how loveable is this human being*. And I tell her about how I once had a spinal tap and she says, *have you ever broken anything?* Then she eats the first leech. Then I eat the second. And we laugh a lot. And it's disgusting. Jen meows now already in the morning. I think this means that she's comfortable, right? We stand in front of the Victoria Secrets in the Termini Train Station and look at all the crap. *It's sexy because there's a sign that says 'sexy'*, says Jen. I see the sign: *sexy now today*. We look at each other in the face and say thank you and all kinds of stuff. And hug a lot. No, *tightly*. And I say, *text me when you get home*. And she says, *OK, Mum*.

We call each other Urch and Leech, interchangeably.

I remember offering to translate the text for her beforehand, but I'm so glad that I didn't.

Confetti Cannon!

Don't be alarmed! It's just questionnaires intended for one of my authors, which I intercepted and adapted. Feel free to catch one and fill it out:

What inspired you to ~~write~~ translate the book?

What research (if any) did you undertake to ~~write~~ translate the book?

Does the <u>book translation</u> contain any personal memories/life events that you are willing to share?

Do you listen to music while you ~~write~~ translate? If so, what music did you listen to while ~~writing~~ translating the book?

Which books inspired you?

Which book do you wish you'd ~~written~~ translated and why?

Describe your typical ~~writing~~ translating routine.

Is there anything else about you or your <u>book translation</u> you'd like to share or think we should know?

Cannon

Can you hold the ladder while I climb inside here?

I'm getting offered the same translation fee after thirteen years as I was when I started. I remember seeing an invoice for a multi-award-winning translator who had been working for thirty years, getting paid what I get paid, what new translators get paid.

Shouldn't we be getting paid on a growing scale, as the Artists' Union recommends for artists? Higher rates based on experience, skill and responsibility? Shouldn't we get paid based on the complexity and actual work time required, not paid by the word (texts aren't made of words, they're made of sentences, paragraphs, chapters and wholes of variable difficulty!).

Shouldn't we be getting paid some kind of *danger money* for this job? Shouldn't all commissioned freelancers? I mean, at least the same as everyone else who has a salaried job in the same field? We have no paid holiday, no sick pay. When I took time off to grieve, to have IVF, when I had burnout, depression, that was all my own time and money. We have to conduct our own training, and we don't get promotions or bonuses. We work unsociable hours and are isolated from the rest of the workforce. We don't have a manager or supervisor and are solely responsible for the whole project up until completion, for the happiness of all involved parties, often being a go-between or even mediator between authors and editor. We often don't get any credit for our work, even though one of our biggest jobs is making ourselves stand out and reminding people we exist. There's actually currently a movement to credit stunt people and have awards to acknowledge the invisible yet highly creative work they do.

It's claustrophobic inside a cannon, isn't it? It's very dark.

Light the fuse! Did you light it? Actually, I think I forgot to do the risk assessment. What do you mean the spark went out anyway?

L98 – The Metamorphosis

On the walls you'll see illustrations from a graphic novel adaptation of Franz Kafka's *The Metamorphosis*.

In the centre of the room, you'll find a desk that is actually a seesaw built for eight people. If one side is up, the other side is down. Take a seat.

I was twenty-five and had just finished my master's when I got the job as Press and PR Coordinator at a German cultural centre in London.

I had no experience, but I was full of enthusiasm and really wanted to put my interest in Anglo-German cultural relations into practice. I brought each of my interviewers a copy of my magazine *Verfreundungseffekt*. At my interview, the director, deputy director and other members of senior staff were very friendly. The first half of the interview was in English, and I did well, but when it turned to German, I could only manage a few stock phrases I had learnt for the interview. Somehow, I beat the other eleven candidates for the job.

When I started and asked what my job entailed specifically, no one could tell me – not the director, whom I reported to directly and who said they were too busy, nor the deputy, who I never saw. The job description had been vague, and when I opened the Word document titled 'Handover' on the empty computer desktop in my office, there was only a third of a page of bullet points that would barely take up a day, let alone a week. When I asked the director if there was anything I could be getting on with straight away, they shouted at me to get on with it, and I never asked again.

I was left to my own devices. I made meetings with heads of departments to see if they needed me to work on anything, and none of them went anywhere. I would offer to write press releases and contact the press about projects, but colleagues would say they were too niche and not to bother. I would casually ask what my former colleague had worked on, but no one knew.

I'd end up in the middle of nowhere for meetings I'd arranged that were vaguely connected to my job, or with people I had actually managed to have a conversation with at one of our events, in the hope it would lead to projects I could impress my betters with and as a reason to get out of the office. Sometimes they would be awkward and pointless right from the beginning – on at least two occasions the man I was meeting thought it was a date. I once ended up in the offices of a local paper having a meeting about advertising rates – a normal interaction for someone who is head of press and PR – but in the knowledge that I had no budget with which to take out an ad. I went from a spritely newbie to a nervous wreck with a knot in my stomach within a couple of months.

I had no direction, no budget, no clue. So I did all the proofreading and translation needed in-house. I set up the Twitter account. I trawled news sites for stories on Anglo-German cultural projects and saved the links in a Word file that no one would ever look at. The first time I did send out a press release, which I had spent a week crafting, about ninety per cent of the emails came back – the press database I'd inherited was years out of date.

During a rare one-on-one meeting with the director, they openly laughed in the middle of me speaking and said, 'Sorry, it's just that you look the same age as my children' (who were teenagers). Someone from outside the institute came in for a meeting with me and the director and said in front of many colleagues that I looked like a schoolgirl. During an appraisal, the deputy director looked at me from across their desk, gave a big sigh, and said that they had all expected such great things from me, and yet... When I asked what exactly they had expected, they couldn't tell me.

I would sit in the weekly meetings and wait to be addressed. If I offered an idea out of turn, everyone would look at me like I had just made a fool of myself. The great irony was that I was in a German workplace and one of only two English people, so should have been immersed completely in German, but because I was in an office on my own I rarely had a chance to practise my German other than in meetings or in the lift (for nearly the whole time I worked there, when colleagues would ask, 'Haben Sie Feierabend?' on the way down at the end of the day, I thought they were asking if I was going out to party (Feier = celebration/party, Abend = evening) and would reply no, I was just going home, when they were in fact just asking if I was clocking off for the day.

The best projects I got to work on were translating interviews with artists for the director's vanity project, and translating the subtitles for a film being shown at the institute, plus translating the captions for an exhibition of artwork from a graphic novel adaptation of *The Metamorphosis* being shown in The Library on the floor below.

While I languished on the third floor feeling useless and foolish, I knew that a magazine called *New Books in German*, which promoted German-language literature to UK and US publishers, was edited out of The Library on the second floor. I had entered their emerging translator competition while working in a clothes shop in Brighton when still in the first year of my master's, for which entrants had to translate a sample from Gregor Hens's *Nikotin* for a place at an advanced workshop with a professional literary translator, but I hadn't been selected.

An internship came up at the magazine. I applied, once again bringing a copy of *Verfreundungseffekt*. I got it. To my third-floor colleagues' confusion, I worked four mornings a week on their floor as the PR coordinator, and a few afternoons downstairs as a magazine intern. After interning for three months, assisting for the course of one issue, the editor, Charlotte Ryland, asked if I wanted to take over as editor for a year (it would turn into two) while she was on maternity leave. After months of feeling useless and being underused, having been patronised and isolated, someone was showing me complete belief and trust.

For each issue, I commissioned articles and interviews and nearly a hundred book or 'reader' reports, and chaired editorial and committee meetings with agents, literary translators I idolised like Anthea Bell, Katy Derbyshire, Jamie Bulloch and Shaun Whiteside, and cultural attachés from the German-speaking embassies and other cultural centres. I corresponded with dozens of German-language rights agents so they would send us their best books for consideration, then went to the London Book Fair and Frankfurt Book Fair for meetings with them. I organised receptions to launch the magazines, and I arranged international distribution (something that I found so stressful my face went numb the first time I attempted it, and I made a mental note to myself that I would never get that stressed again – I came up with the mantra 'No one is going to die' for whenever I lost perspective while editing, writing or, later on, translating). In the time it would take to get the lift from the third to the second floor, I went from a belittled and undervalued office worker to a respected and challenged magazine editor.

Two of the most satisfying happenings during an editorial meeting were, first, when one of my senior colleagues from upstairs asked to join one of the meetings out of interest, and they watched absolutely stunned as I chaired and harnessed a meeting of twenty publishing professionals, and second when one of the regular committee members I was most intimidated by, Theodora Danek, invited me to become the freelance literary curator at the Austrian cultural institute after my time as editor and as PR coordinator had come to an end.

I would go on to bring together a set designer, a director and an actor to recreate a detective's office and murderer's lair and perform a few scenes from a German crime novel translated by Jamie Lee Searle, and commission a range of creative practitioners to make ceramics, costumes, film and sound pieces as 'translations' of a short story I'd translated for a dedicated exhibition I called 'Translation as Firework' (I stuck the vinyl on the wall myself, with some help). This institute, just around the corner, felt like home, and Theodora and the Director encouraged me to push my creativity and ambition, and to be confident about how I wanted to present translation to the public.

I never wanted to work in an office again.

Z23–A23 – Busts of Charlotte Ryland and Theodora Danek

Over here are white marble busts of Charlotte Ryland and Theodora Danek, my friends and former colleagues, with a garland of flowers on their heads. Charlotte saw something in me and gave me access to and control of a whole world, allowing me to learn everything there is to know about promoting and publishing translations, even though I was young and inexperienced. Theodora trusted me to curate events and translate authors I invited to attend, including my own future translator, Carolina Schutti. Theodora and I collaborated on a translation of a novel excerpt, and she edited my translation of Michelle Steinbeck. She is the one I go to if I have a translation question. Lydia Davis sometimes calls those she asks about translation issues 'native informants'. This feels a bit spy-y to me, a bit cold. Theodora is my friend and collaborator, and I would be nowhere without her.

Y6 – Translator Dreamhouse

Gather around this table-sized glass case holding what might just look like a model of a bog-standard open-plan office.

I lived in a warehouse in Stoke Newington with my partner and four to six friends for over five years in order to afford to live in London and get into literary translation and writing. A few of us plus some additional people worked in a shared studio in a former Scout hut, a room that just about fit eight desks in facing pairs. I had so much focus. I was surrounded by illustrators, artists, photographers, essayists, producers, all working with great concentration on creative pursuits that, like me, meant interpreting a brief and making something of it. I could work from 9 a.m. to midnight, bolstered by the camaraderie. We would have naturally occurring coffee breaks; my deskmate Sam, an illustrator, and I would walk to the local bakery for a freshly made egg and cress roll and a coffee at lunchtime. This was where I translated a few of my first books. But then the rent went up, with a likelihood of it going up again, and I had to move out; the others followed not long after.

Looking at the next generation coming up, I see that though we weren't as lucky as the generation before us, we were still very lucky. The comedian Stewart Lee, who lived round the corner, spoke on the radio about how back in the day people could live in squats or on cheap rent while mastering an art, could afford to go out and feel inspired at things others had put on, but how now everyone just worries about paying rent.

My flatmates and I were all getting older and were all in long-term relationships, and the time came for us to live separately. Richard and I moved to a flat in Brixton for not as much money as we should have been paying because our landlady used to be a campaigner for fair rent and knew that as a freelance writer-translator and a freelance artist-creative facilitator, we wouldn't be able to afford to live in London otherwise. I tried having a desk in a shared studio locally, but it was expensive and the atmosphere wasn't the same. The final straw was when it got broken into and someone's laptop got stolen, and when a rat ate my bag of nuts and pooped all over my desk, which I was asked to come in and clean up on my way to the award ceremony of a translation prize I was shortlisted for.

So I decided to work from home, and for five years it felt so hard, so unproductive. Translation and writing had always meant working solo, but working solo with other people. Even though the rent was cheaper than it should have been, we had to leave London. At least we managed it for a while and still have threads of connection.

I've been rewatching *Mad Men* and feeling envious of the Sterling Cooper advertising agency's offices. The natural light pouring into the bustling typing pool, the bright private offices with their views. The art department on top of one another in one room, surrounded by sketches, working frantically at large slanted desks. The telephone exchange girls crammed together in a broom cupboard, connecting people. I'm also envious of the coffee, sandwich and Danish stand in the middle of it all, where employees can pop by for lunch or a pick-me-up.

I've created my own version, my own take. Each office contains a translator, their name in chic block lettering on the door. The typing pool are assistants who chase down our invoices, proofread our translations, research hard-to-track-down words. We have conference rooms where we invite publishers to pitch our translations to as a group. We loll around in one another's offices, on the sofas or perched on desks or lying on the floor, cracking one another's translation problems, or sharing our issues with editors or authors or other translators (something we do now, but too rarely, by travelling and convening at the same conference, the same event, or at one of our houses to debrief the last year or few years). There's a stand that sells coffee, gingerbread people that represent all the translators in the office, delicious sandwiches, snacks galore. There's Rosalind Harvey, Ruth Ahmedzai Kemp, Sophie Hughes, Annie McDermott, Saskia Vogel, Polly Barton. I know it's not possible; we all live in different towns, cities, countries, on different continents.

We'd all be on liveable salaries, paid for by a consortium of publishers and arts funding. Publishers or the government – never unethical sponsors or covert corporations masquerading as art orgs – would all pay to keep us on collective retainer (stranger and similar things have happened elsewhere). We'd all be happy and have the upper hand through our collective power; when things were bad we'd go on strike, lock the doors, turn off the Internet and take the phones of the hook. When things were good, we'd have monthly dinners and a Christmas party.

It wouldn't have to be this fancy, it could be an old Scout hut with a café nearby, or a set of artists' studios portioned out with plasterboard that doesn't reach the ceiling and a shared kitchenette, a couple of chairs with bent legs, but even that now feels out of reach, extravagant.

Though it doesn't exist as a job, I wonder what it would be like if publishers just took on translators in-house. We would be employed and have a desk in an office, where we would work on translations only for that one house, read foreign-language submissions for them, represent the publisher abroad, go and woo authors (I mean, we do this already, mostly unpaid and unacknowledged). Book designers used to always be in-house, didn't they, before things started changing. But I know things are going in the opposite direction – creatives have gone from having a home together to being out in the cold. I like being able to be on my own, but sometimes aloneness turns into loneliness. Ninety per cent of the same letters, very different meaning.

What, wait, how... how have we ended up back at the replica of my desk? Who set the dimmer switch for the fake window to 'Dusk in January'? It's very quiet here, isn't it?

Q7 – Feedback & Complaints Station

On this stand are a selection of wall-mounted telephones where you can listen to feedback and complaints I've received.

<u>On the peach-coloured phone</u>, you can hear the fellow students on my postgraduate course in German Studies complain about Germans and Austrians:

> *They're awful. When I had my year abroad, I couldn't stand them, they're so annoying.*

They loved learning the language, they loved studying the same German writers who had been dead for decades, but disliked German people, a weird fetishisation whereby German is solely a field of study. I couldn't understand it. They wanted to analyse Germans and their culture and language. To be honest, that's what studying can do, and it's what I had wanted to do before living in Munich. Studying can objectify things to such a degree that you forget these people once lived, that Germanness is fluid and alive. You even forget that German culture is living, not what is in history books. That German-language books are being published every day, something I barely registered about English-language books at age twenty-three. When you study books that aren't wholly contemporary, you think all literature happened in the past.

I wanted to do something that showed a love and appreciation of German culture, and I wanted it to be about now. I thought of all my British, American, Australian friends who appreciated something German, and vice versa. I made a magazine, *Verfreundungseffekt*, a neologism inspired by Brecht's Verfremdungseffekt, alienation or distancing effect (it has multiple translations, I prefer to name all of them to give you a fuller effekt), transformed into friendation or bringing-closer effect.

<u>On the red phone</u>, you can listen to the complaints I received working in a call centre for a now defunct fashion brand, in English and German:

Wo ist meine Lieferung? Where is my delivery?

My colleague S, who handled the French-language complaints, would listen to *my* complaints about wanting to do something else with my life. We would take walks around the block in Soho complaining about our sexist, homophobic, creepy man-baby boss, who paid us the same as our monolingual colleagues because, according to him, we knew the foreign languages, so how could it be more work?

S wanted to be a curator. I told her about *Verfreundungseffekt*, and she jumped into action. She found an empty launderette and asked the council if we could use it for a week. She helped me plan an exhibition and a launch event for the magazine. Friends' bands played German-language cover songs. The photos and illustrations from the magazine were put up on the walls.

A couple of years later I brought out the second issue (at this point I realised that Austria and Switzerland ought to be included; it took me this long to become inclusive – German-language culture, not German culture) and had another launch, this time in a gallery, with bands and readings again.

Philip Oltermann, the German affairs correspondent for a major newspaper, came. He had seen a post about the launch on social media. A few weeks later, he recommended me to his publisher, Faber & Faber, to translate Wim Wenders's essay collection *The Pixels of Paul Cézanne*, which he largely wrote in poem-like columns. I think of them as prose poems.

On the purple telephone, you can hear complaints I received from reviewers and readers about my translation of Wim Wenders's book, which I've turned into poems:

Michelangelo would never
from a review in *The Spectator*

Might some of these problems be down to Jen Calleja's shaky translation?

There is no Mann movie called 'Man from the West',
though – as the rest of the essay makes clear –
there is one called *Man of the West*.

Even after the stroke that eventually killed him,
Michelangelo Antonioni would never have said 'doppo'
though he might have said *dopo* or
since he and Wenders were in a restaurant together, *doppio*.

And while we no longer frown upon sentences
that end with a preposition,
we can't just dump any old
preposition there.

When Calleja has Wenders ask himself
'What's *happening* to the people in front of my camera?
What does their dignity consist of?'
she only confirms
Werner Herzog's suspicion
that 'film is not the art of scholars
but illiterates'.

Wim would never
from an email

I.
A friendly note to say something about prepositions and
 geography.

On page 37, you have the house 'at Cape Cod'
but local usage trumps grammar
when it comes to geography;
so, no one from Cape Cod would ever say 'at'

it is always 'on' – as in

I'll be 'on the Cape'.
The 'at' would come in into [sic] play
if I referred to my house –
'I'll be at the Cape house for a month.'

So far as I can tell
the shape of the land causes all this –
I deal with Baja California a lot
& it has the same issues as Cape Cod.

One is 'in' Italy, 'at the cottage',
or 'on Baja', but never
'at Baja', or 'in' Baja.

My suggestion is to ask locals how they say it
when dealing with or translating tales about
islands & peninsulas

and also to note that there is
a typo on page
81.

That's it.

I tried replying to tell the person who had sent the latter that Wim
had written that essay in English himself, but the email bounced
back from the ticket office of a Canadian opera house.

The blue phone allows you to pick it up and scream either,

Did every person in publishing go to Oxbridge?

or, quoting the German-British writer Isabel Waidner,

Support non-Oxbridge talent

and it will relay to a speaker at the other end of the fair.

On the yellow phone you can hear a translator saying over and over that

It is uncouth for translators to complain.

What's your complaint?

K5343 – Before the Law

Here we have *Before the Law* (2024), an artwork by Poppy Whatmore titled after Kafka's parable 'Before the Law', which is, basically, about how impenetrable the law is for the common man. As you can see, the artwork comprises a portion of a gate, the white picket fence kind of gate but painted light pink, with one blue tube and one green tube twining through the slats. It is leaning against the wall of this stand. Beside it is a pile of rubble with a window frame propped against it.

My school was knocked down a few years after I left (represented here by a pile of bricks, and the rusty window frame that literally fell out of the side of the school one day). I finished my A-levels in 2005, and in 2008 the then Secretary of State, Ed Balls, announced that my school was 'failing' because fewer than thirty per cent of students managed to achieve A–C grades at GCSE. The year previous to that, only twenty-three per cent of pupils attained five or more GCSEs at Grade C or above including English and Maths, roughly half the national average.

I daydreamed a lot, but I had an active mind, I practically lived inside my own head. I both didn't feel motivated or stretched, and found tasks hard to parse and pointless. I could never comprehend grammar, I still cannot tell you what an adverb is, but I could write detailed stories aged nine (I was placed in a group that could skip assembly to write – I thought at the time that it was a reward, but I think now it was because I couldn't concentrate in class or during assemblies). My teachers had consistently said at parents' evenings that I was bright, if underachieving, and I (and probably my parents) assumed that this is what they told all the students.

I wanted some form of verification of this underlying but never proven feeling that I might be capable of thinking in a specific way; that perhaps the reason I found school so monotonous was because I saw things differently. I ended up signing up for an IQ test aged sixteen – a test full of patterns and sequences – and scored in the top two per cent of the country. My parents didn't say anything, it seemed to make them uncomfortable; my mum rescinded the bet she made that I wouldn't pass it. I didn't tell anyone else. Whether I'm smart or not has always been a family mystery. *It's not your fault you're clever*, my dad said recently while we were walking, and we laughed our heads off at my major fault.

As a child, my parents were unable to help me with homework, and they didn't read to us; they had left school young and preferred to leave us to it. I wondered what it would have been like to have parents who could help or offer an opinion, to whom I could show my school work and later my draft university essays and my creative writing for feedback, like other people did; I remember reading about a translator who could show their parents and grandparents their work because they not only knew both languages but had all been in literature in some way. I daydreamed about being able to do this with my family.

But I appreciate now that I learnt from a very young age, when I was still aged in single digits, to listen to what I thought about what I was reading, what I was writing. I only owned a few books growing up, which meant I read and reread them; this was a normal reading process for me, reading the book, rereading it, over and over. Just as I do when I translate, when I write. Every story deserves twelve reads. I can handle those twelve reads.

And when I had to write, I was aware that I was the one who would have to excavate and rebuild the text, all by myself. Sometimes to a fault, filling cracks that kept reopening, rotating the building plans this way and that in despair, when I could have asked for a second opinion, a third opinion, a fourth. I could spend hours in my bedroom drawing, writing, and never seek validation, and now I sit at home at my desk and I'm not intimidated at writing or translating a book and having only my own standards to meet. If I always had that compulsion to show a parent, I doubt I would have written or translated a thing. Your translations can never be signed off fully, not by the author or the editor, it's up to you to be satisfied, knowing that you worked – pretty much – completely on your own, and I can be at peace with letting things go.

When it was time to apply for university, it was put forward that I should apply to study (or *read*) English at Oxbridge (someone had to explain to me that this meant Oxford and Cambridge, and that Oxbridge wasn't a third university; I picked Cambridge as I just preferred the word over 'Oxford'). My school had only had a handful of students go to Oxbridge, none for six or seven years. I didn't have a say in the matter.

This time is vivid to me because I felt helpless, confused, resentful, under a numbing pressure, and received zero support to navigate or prepare for the process. When I got offered an interview, I was taken to a classroom by my English teachers and advised to say I had read widely outside school (I hadn't), not to tell the interviewers that my favourite author was Terry Pratchett, and not to let on that my parents read the *Daily Mail*. I was also encouraged to say that I had a difficult home life due to my mum's mental illness, as this might give me 'more of a chance'.

It was an early lesson in hiding who I was, my qualities, if I wanted to fit in. But I knew, even at seventeen, that if you had to prove your intelligence and worth by means other than what you did – your actions, your work – then it was all a sham, an illusion; we learn about the emperor's new clothes as little children, don't we? It's always seemed to me like a self-fulfilling prophecy. I didn't want to go to Cambridge because I didn't want to go through university only for someone to say, should I achieve what I wanted to achieve, that going there had got me to where I am today. No one was going to take the credit for my work and who I was, even if people yearn for some kind of official proof, for certificates, your life's history.

For their part, my parents seemed very uneasy about me applying. They worried that there would probably be a lot of extra costs, the fancy robes and clothes, the extracurricular activities. Going to university was already a leap; applying to Cambridge felt like a sad chasm, a tragedy. Their reaction, I'm sure, also coloured my experience, but ultimately I wasn't interested right from the start.

I went because I felt I couldn't say no, flunked the first part (a sit-down exam I couldn't fathom, and an interview in front of a panel who seemed to speak in riddles), and by the second later that afternoon I was done with the whole thing. I told the head of the college I'd applied to that I loved Terry Pratchett (he felt the same) and that my parents read the *Daily Mail*, that I did not want to go to Cambridge and wanted to go to Goldsmiths because they offered modules in creative writing (he encouraged this choice). He did put me forward to other colleges at the university as he felt I should have the option if I changed my mind, but I never checked to see if any of them offered me a place. Getting an unconditional offer from Goldsmiths trumped the whole experience.

I've faced a lot of people calling Goldsmiths, where I did my undergraduate degree in English and media, 'a joke'. I went to Goldsmiths because it offered creative writing, absolutely, but also because it didn't intimidate me like other universities did. When I got the interview at Cambridge, staying overnight in a stone tower at the college did not feel exciting, it terrified me. Cloisters everywhere! When I walked down the black-and-white-floored corridors of Goldsmiths (hence the white and black tiles on the floor here), I felt relief. It felt like my school. It's seen as a joke because, like most universities that mainly teach the arts, it's seen as pretentious, a word to undermine places that take art, creativity, experiment and questioning seriously. We felt like writers, artists, musicians every day, from the first day, and not just in thrall to those in the past, where the arts were everywhere, and beloved.

In spite of Goldsmiths feeling more comfortable than other universities I'd visited, I still felt out of my depth. I was the first person in my whole family to go to university, or do post-sixteen academic education, and was feeling so overwhelmed I decided to sign up for the university counselling service in my first term. In my first session with the counsellor, a former English teacher, he asked me why I was putting so much pressure on myself. I told him that I wanted to do well at university and that I wanted to become a writer. *I'd forget all about that*, he told me with a laugh, *don't you think you're having delusions of grandeur?*

I learnt a lot at Goldsmiths, read things that changed my life, engaged my critical thinking, and I felt at home in the interdisciplinarity that was encouraged. It's also where I started my first band and started writing for the university magazine and friends' zines and publications.

After finishing my degree, I knew that I wanted to eventually do a master's in German. I was finally ready to admit to myself that it was what I wanted to do, even if I was scared, but because I only had an A-level in German there weren't many options.

University College London offered a postgraduate degree where an A-level in the language you wanted to study was sufficient. I applied and was offered an interview. The interviewer, head of department I assume, asked me if I'd had 'fun' at Goldsmiths, and, looking at the first-class degree I'd achieved, reassured me *there's additional help on hand if you need it*.

I would have to sit a German language exam there and then, he said, so I sat at an old computer in his office with a boiling mug of tea, filled to the brim and with the bag still in, floating like a miniature corpse in a white flowing dress (here's a replica of the mug of tea, but five times the size, steaming, here to the right of the gate, don't get too close, it's permanently hot, letters rise to the surface before sinking back down, like in a lava lamp). It was a multiple-choice test and took about forty-five minutes – most of the interview.

I received an email from the interviewer a few weeks later informing me that I had failed the language exam, but that he would allow me a place *at his discretion*. I felt so ashamed and wondered if I should do the degree at all. It was what I wanted to do, though, so I accepted on a part-time basis. My parents gave me half the fee for the first year and my grandparents the other half, and I worked four and half days a week to pay for the second year.

In my very first seminar, the tutor said that we would go around the room saying which school we had attended, and which university. I saw this immediately for what it was, and played along. Many of the other students said posh-sounding schools and prestigious universities, and every time someone mentioned they had studied at Oxford, I kid you not, the tutor made an involuntary/voluntary high-pitched noise of approval in their throat – *Hm!* When one student had said that they had attended a certain Oxford college, the tutor couldn't contain themselves and said that they had also gone to and taught at that college and would love to speak with the student afterwards.

When it was my turn, I felt really pleased to say in full, *King's Manor Community College and Sixth Form Centre and Goldsmiths College*. But I couldn't concentrate for the rest of the seminar, and I felt a kind of rage-shame afterwards,

About six weeks into the course, I opted to meet with my personal tutor and said that I was having doubts about my abilities, especially after failing the language exam, to which she replied that there was no such language exam, it was not a requirement, and no one else had had to take it.

Opened gate, closed gate.

I was nearly at the end of my master's when I decided that I wanted to become a literary translator. But I wasn't sure how people got commissioned to translate books. Many of the translators I had researched had attended top schools and top universities in the UK and the USA, and I believed that this was what was required, that there would be no way of getting into translating literature, that it was over before it had begun. I would comb through bios on websites and in the backs of translated books to glean what kind of person I needed to be to be a translator, and I didn't seem to match up. Their biographies seemed to be the same as English-language authors', the same as editors'; they all seemed to be in the same closed circles.

I was feeling isolated and decided to get on social media – Twitter, specifically. I found lots of literary translators and writers, but also book and magazine editors. I was no longer standing outside the building trying to get in, I was in an infinitely long corridor lined with doors with editors' names on them and little post boxes outside. Twitter was a back door to get through the gate.

I started using Twitter as a rolling CV. If I translated something for someone, I posted about it. If I had been reading an interesting book in German, I shared it. Editors at publishing houses who had followed me back asked me to do things for them off the back of what I had done, reading books for them and writing reports, trying out for translations. I could also contact editors directly in response to translation queries, or offer to pitch them potential translation projects. I was judged solely on my work, on whether I could do the job. Everything I did was put right at the top of the web pile on the desktops of commissioning editors and programmers.

Not only that, but the translators I followed would generously share interesting articles and give advice. I would stand on the edges of conversations happening in real time that revealed so much about the practice and the day-to-day. Before long, I was part of those conversations. I looked forward to opening Twitter in the morning, when everyone would be at their desk at the same time and all the chatter would begin, carrying on throughout the day. I felt like we were all together, like a big shared office. We decried when one of us wasn't credited in book reviews, and celebrated when one of us was.

On social media, I found I could perform myself in a certain way that in effect sometimes flattened who I was. Over time I drafted a palette of vocabulary and a way to speak that was my Twitter voice. It didn't sound like me, necessarily, because what I sounded like online, my turns of phrase and the slang I used, suddenly sounded performative, like a character. In fact, those writers, editors and translators I knew who were from middle- and upper-middle-class backgrounds 'put on' a voice that sounded far more like how I sounded in real life, while I felt like I had to sound less-than-myself.

I feel like I'm a translator of the Internet and social media age – I wouldn't have found connections without social media, I wouldn't have been able to research and have access to knowledge and a range of online dictionaries without the Internet. But the time of social media creating access, a period that lasted about a decade, seems to now be over – editors have abandoned Twitter, so have more experienced translators. Will things return to how they were in the beforetime?

Will the doors close again, so that it's *who you know* and not *what you know*? There are now degrees in literary translation – will that be the entryway, like the way art and creative writing degrees have now become the currency of the creative industries? I don't know if I would be able to make it now, and that means there are many coming up now who are possibly in the same position.

Swinging gate.

A couple of years ago, I was invited to take part in a translation duel at a literary festival in the UK. A fancy festival. I was in the green room talking with a couple of other writers I did and did not know, when a well-known poet approached our group. I wish I was joking when I say that after introducing themselves, they asked, 'Who here went to Oxford?' Everyone put up their hand apart from me. One of the writers said, 'I did, but I hated it.' The poet replied, 'Oh really, that's interesting, I'd like to hear more,' and then the circle closed around them, physically leaving me out.

I left the room, my eyes almost rolling out of my head, so glad that I would never be that embarrassing.

When I point out that others have had more privileged upbringings or educations, it's not because I'm saying I'm more entitled or they're less entitled. I'm just pointing out that people from a wide range of experiences, personalities, backgrounds, can make great art like translations, that privilege can be a smokescreen or a free pass. Here's the fog machine, right on cue. The proof should be in the pudding, but some people don't even get to make the pudding or have their pudding judged. Pudding anyone? Do take a bowl from the tray being passed around, it's a jam roly-poly and custard.

Why keep going when there have been so many times when it feels like I should have given up? It is a form of stubbornness for sure. I want to disprove the rules, I've been playing my own game. I just keep going to see what happens if I don't turn back.

C3 – Folly

On this enormous stand, one that's taking up far too much space in my opinion, is a folly that looks like a small castle, no more than the height and proportions of a largish room. Stand on this exact spot, this X on the ground, and view it from this angle.

This folly was 3D-printed, it was created in one piece in three seconds by robots. It has the appearance of the real thing, but if you look closely, there are strange details. The turrets are the wrong colour, the bricks are only drawn on. Every wall is slightly different, like it's many bits of castle from different locations and time periods stuck together. It's got no foundations and could be toppled easily. It's empty inside.

Read the little sign stuck in the ground next to it: HISTORY OF FOLLY. None found.

Now, if we walk slightly around its 'walls', we'll see that there's a real castle behind it, very similar to this one. This castle has had its foundations dug, the bricks were made and laid by hand. There is moss, the castle has been lived in.

The folly is blocking our view. The folly wasn't anyone's long-term project or way of exerting their energy, their pleasure and profession.

The author Catherine Lacey complained to the *New Yorker* after they began using AI voices to read out their articles, because it did the writing such disservice. Someone else pointed out that in one story, the AI gets the intonation wrong, turning a sarcastic comment into an earnest query. This non-voice, this sound, makes audible that AI cannot read.

I've started to be asked by publishers to edit 'translations' created by 'artificial intelligence'. You can't edit these things that only have the appearance of a text; they're an obstacle to a real translation built from the ground up, blocking the view.

Spotlight!

Ah, the roving spotlight has landed on me! *Yes!!!*

Is this Fair all a bit much? Do I seem a bit self-obsessed?

A writer recently wrote:

> As much as I love literature in translation, and am thankful to
> anyone doing that work, I can't help feeling that a lot of the
> most prominent contemporary *literaryfiction* [sic] translators
> are a bunch of narcissistic cunts. Or at least they behave like
> that on social media. Which is the same. You might quote me
> on this.

I have quoted them on this, I had it made into a tapestry, navy
blue with silver thread surrounded by golden stars, and it's hung up
on that stand over there, N8.

I think they're referring to the fact that translators seem to have
become very vocal about their work and circumstances. They always
have been, though with less possibility for platform and exposure.

My partner Richard wrote a book about being a freelance facilitator
for art and music projects supporting young people with learning
disabilities, a role he has done for twenty years. We have talked for
hours about how we write about our different roles, often returning
to the question: why should the mediator speak?

In both our jobs, we are expected to be invisible. In both our jobs,
we think we should be both invisible and not invisible, and that this
invisibility/visibility is for ethical reasons. We want the creative
person we're supporting to take centre stage, that is key. But we also
believe that in the interest of transparency, people should know who
is facilitating, mediating and representing the work and the person
who made it. We want outsiders to know that there are different
approaches to our work, not one way. We also think we need to be
visible so other organisations and publishers can find us to involve

us in their projects, and to highlight issues with pay and working conditions.

By talking about myself and my experience of translation, maybe it can also show how someone gets into this niche, opaque work, so more people can find their own path into it or see how they might have already started preparing for it, way back. Every time I talk about what I do, I also hope to draw attention to translation in general, and all literary translators. I don't want to be a celebrity, the queen of translation, I prefer to stick with the group. I've seen what happens in D.I.Y. punk – sometimes a whiff of fame and money can make people drop the scene and the rest of the band, and maybe some translators will be tempted to be the go-to person, to become a brand, to hog the limelight.

I was once a very quiet person, but I was radicalised by watching a panel discussion where panellists said that translators should work with *real writers* to create the best translation, and that the translation of literature should be crowdsourced, with translators chipping in a few paragraphs and getting paid accordingly. I couldn't let this slide, so I had to become one of those cuntish translators who talk about themselves all the time.

I pitched a column to an online literary journal that had previously published my poetry and they gave me one. I wired in my own spotlight.

As with any made-invisible group – especially a group that is badly paid – the moment they start speaking out, it's deemed too much, too visible, turn out the lights!

U23 – Overcrowded Book Launch

The stand is surrounded by balloons, cheap wine is being poured into plastic cups on a low, glass-topped table. It will shortly be announced that the world English-language rights to Maltese author Loranne Vella's short story collection *mill-bieb 'il ġewwa* have been sold to Praspar Press. I founded Praspar with my friend Kat to publish Maltese authors in English and English translation. The book will be our second publication.

Kat, who is Maltese and works in UK publishing, came to find me at an event I was chairing in a bookshop after spotting my very Maltese surname attached to one of my translations. Being credited for my translation helped her find me. She decided, miraculously, that she had to meet me. After the event, she approached me to introduce herself. I had never met another Maltese or part-Maltese person in the UK before. I clearly remember that I felt a wave of warm feeling towards Kat, and we agreed to meet up then and there.

At our first meeting, in the bar of a fancy cinema (whose heavy grey-blue velvet curtains run around the walls of the stand, there's a popcorn machine gently *pup-pupping* in the corner, help yourself to it with a Praspar-branded box), we started talking about our connections to Malta. Kat was born and grew up there, speaks Maltese and still has strong connections there. My dad was born there but we rarely visited; I was born and raised in the UK and can't speak Maltese. We talked about both having played in D.I.Y. bands, about publishing in student magazines. We were united in our disappointment that Maltese literature wasn't reaching the UK. The literature of this small island wasn't getting any interest or attention from publishers. This could be for many reasons, we reasoned: Malta wasn't in the British imagination, editors didn't regularly come across Maltese writing or travel to Malta seeking books, there didn't seem to be any UK-based literary translators from Maltese.

It would take two and a half years from our first meeting for us to finally decide to start a small press, and another year and a half for us to launch it. We asked my friend Patrick, who used to drum in a band that my old band played and toured with, and who is now a freelance book designer, to typeset the books and create the covers. Though we wouldn't be paid for our work on the press, both Patrick and the translators of the books would be paid through funding we received from the National Book Council of Malta.

As an aside, the D.I.Y. music to D.I.Y. publishing pipeline is a thing – I know so many bands, musicians, record labels who also write and publish. Writing, recording, doing artwork for, pressing and putting out a record and making a book are extremely similar processes. Though in many ways Kat and I don't have much as Praspar – monied backgrounds, connections – we were part of communities that helped us have the belief to be able to do something out of seemingly nothing, through calling in favours and expertise and having experienced the D.I.Y. ethos first-hand. Praspar Press is a D.I.Y. punk publisher in more ways than one.

Kat and I were both aware of the author Loranne Vella. Kat read her short story collection in a weekend, and she said she thought it could be a perfect first full-length publication for our press. As I couldn't read the book myself, I had to completely trust Kat, which wasn't difficult. This was usually my role – convincing an editor or publisher who couldn't read a book in German that the book was good, was right for them, that they should spend time and money bringing it out in English, even though they wouldn't be able to read the whole book until the translation was finished. I also thought back on my impression of Loranne when I chaired a panel discussion she was on at the London Book Fair about Maltese writing in translation. Was this the kind of person I would give my time for, much of it voluntary? I felt that, yes, beyond the matter of the book itself, she seemed like the kind of person I would invest my time in, who would trust me and be open to discussions and collaboration.

In order to lock in the funding from the Book Council by the end of the year, we had to immediately find a translator, but no one came to mind whose work we knew well enough, and the chances were that the translator might not agree to the job at such short notice. We decided that we would translate the book 'in-house' and that Kat would take on the job, even though she had never translated a book before.

People are starting to gather around the cups of wine; the full announcement text is being adhered to the wall of the booth, vinyl letter by vinyl letter. So far it reads: *Praspar Press to publish Loranne Vella's* mill-bieb 'il ġewwa *in English translation*.

Only a handful of works of Maltese literature have been published in English translation in the UK ever. These include two poetry collections by Immanuel Mifsud, which are dancing from springs from the ceiling and bouncing up and down, *boiiing boiiing*. Try and catch one!

The second of these books, *The Play of Waves*, has a translation credit on the cover that intrigues me. Under the author's name and title, separated by what look like two thin drops of blood lying on their side and touching at the drops' full end, it reads:

Translated by Maurice Riordan
Introduction by Charles Briffa

I knew Riordan was an Irish poet, and I thought to myself, amazing, he learnt Maltese and translated this book of poetry. But on turning to the title page, I could already see that this book wasn't what it was purporting to be. Another person had appeared:

Translated by Maurice Riordan
with <u>Maria Grech Ganado</u>
Introduction by Charles Briffa

I flicked to the Translator's Preface at the beginning of the book, where Riordan explains that he first came across Mifsud's poetry in 2004 when he was commissioned to translate a Maltese writer to mark Malta's inclusion in the EU. This is followed by the line: 'Translating *Confidential Reports* (a selection of his poems) was my first encounter with Maltese poetry.' Let me snatch down the other book. *Boiiiing!*

On the front cover it states even more boldly, underneath the title:

translated from the Maltese
by Maurice Riordan

and once more on the title page, someone else accompanies him, the poet I once tried to translate with my Dad:

with <u>Adrian Grima</u>

This is quite a riveting mystery. Back to the preface in the first, *The Play of Waves*. Riordan summarises Mifsud's style and form, reassuring us with his mentions of hendecasyllables, hyperbole, flexible units, free and blank verse. The final paragraph, however, makes me feel a bit dizzy:

> In making these versions, I have relied heavily on the prior work of Maria Grech Ganado – herself a distinguished poet in English and in Maltese – who is uniquely attuned to the complexity and nuance of Mifsud's language. My own contribution has often been minimal, and where I have departed conspicuously from her rendition, no doubt I have risked gratuitous interference with the original.

He continues and ends the preface so:

> My hope, even so, is that I have given voice, at least on occasion, to a poetry of plangent music and vibrant textures; and, more generally, I hope to have roused the curiosity of English readers to the work of this latter-day troubadour – whose gloomy, wayward, excessive poems deserve a wide audience.

These poems became 'versions' and not translations the moment he purposefully altered the actual poem translations, all crafted by Maria Grech Ganado, the person who is actually 'attuned' to Mifsud's work, who would go on to become the inaugural Poet Laureate of Malta a few years later, and whose poetry we later published in one of our anthologies.

If a literary translator said in their translator's preface that they had reached a high standard only 'on occasion' and had put their name to someone else's work, they would be reprimanded, ridiculed, written off as a translator. What has been put in place to allow Riordan to be so brazen? The stakes are low for him: he doesn't really want to be a literary translator, he doesn't want a long-term engagement with Maltese culture and literature. Did he get his few lines on the history of Maltese literature second-hand from Ganado, the first Maltese woman to be a full-time lecturer at the University of Malta, a two-time National Book Prize award winner for poetry, first in Maltese and then in English, too? She doesn't get a preface, by the way. And really, Riordan seems to say, as long as he has drawn attention to Mifsud in some way, won't it all be worthwhile?

I once attended a literary festival where a well-known British poet, who writes in book bios that they are a translator, was invited to talk about translating a foreign-language poet in spite of having worked with a literary translator on the book. Though they put across knowledge as if it had been theirs all along, this wasn't their knowledge and they, like Riordan, had not translated the poems – both belonged to the translator, who had not been invited to the festival because they weren't a well-known figure.

During the pandemic, I watched a panel discussion online where a multi-award-winning poet discussed a translation collaboration they had taken part in. They didn't know the original language, and said that when they read the translations prepared by the translator, they would often catch something where the translator had strayed from their role of creating 'literal', 'neutral' translations for the poet to play with – the literary translations were too musical, in other words, too literary or well done, not flat-seeming or bland, which seemed to spoil the illusion of 'translating' for the poet. Not only did the translator have to translate the poems, they also had to act as an interpreter between the writer of the poems and the poet brought in to 'translate'. The actual translator wasn't invited to discuss the translation process at this panel.

Another poet recently said in an interview that when they translate, they often do it with a translator and the author.

I don't think translation means what they think it means. I wouldn't describe these writers as translators, I would say they zhuzh up translators' translations, who could do a fine enough job without them. In trying to 'create exposure' for foreign-language authors (and, I'll say it, themselves), it makes translators *more invisible* and seemingly incapable of doing their jobs.

Other poets have put their counterparts from abroad through translation software, or cut up and combined translators' work to make their own 'translation', or created loose versions based on one or more translations, or simply made things up based on a couple of words they know in the foreign language. They, too, seem to think it's worthwhile because the foreign-language writers are getting some kind of attention, even if the work isn't strictly translation, even if the work doesn't make it through.

If translation is a kind of listening, these writers are only really listening to themselves. They tell stories they perhaps really believe are their own because they've forgotten where they got them. I think of the poet Chen Chen, who said regarding writing poetry: 'better, I think, when I work on a poem, to believe I have something to learn rather than something to say.' This is the same for translating poetry.

Though the above poets aren't translators, this is not to say that these poets have given nothing to the translations, or that experimenting with generating new poems from other poems is worthless. These poets might have helped find solutions or brought in counter-ideas – this is the wonder of collaboration. Simply having more than one person involved in any project means that things can be seen from multiple angles. They are acting as editors, but they always need translators to be able to weigh up edits against the original. We need to be able to announce when something is a version – creative writing – and when something really is a translation. It's the fair thing to do.

Why were all those poets given such prominent credit, other than for the on-sight draw for a reader in a bookshop over a little-known translator, who, if credited more often, could become the draw themselves? If we get behind what's happening, are translation projects more likely to get funded here in the UK if a famous writer is involved? Are international translation projects reliant on the involvement of an English-speaking writer? Is this what undermines translators, over-privileges English-speakers?

Who really translated Immanuel Mifsud?
Who is really translating Loranne Vella?
This is a pressing issue because the vinyl letters need to go up, and the technicians need an answer. Let's see...

Translated by Kat Storace and Jen Calleja

Kat will be translating the whole book, and I know how much work goes into translating a book. We will be working together, we will be collaborating on it. But Kat will be the one actually recreating the book in English from Maltese in the first instance. She knows the language and culture intimately and will be putting English-language sentences to paper.

My role will mainly be to read her translation as an editor of English prose, as a first reader of the translation, and to mentor her in ways to approach her translation, the limits and boundaries and giving her permission to try different things. I will ask questions, and she will know the answers. She knows where the stresses in the sentences seem to lie when she reads the stories. It would be disingenuous of me to say that how I might read the text would have the same legitimacy. I will not be rewriting Kat's translation. It doesn't seem fair for me to claim to hold hands with Kat while she holds hands with the text, with the 'Translated by'.

Translated by Jen Calleja

What!

or:

Translated by Jen Calleja
with Kat Storace

Absurd!

The technicians are getting restless. The letters go up.

Translated by Kat Storace

Let's raise a plastic cup of wine or juice to Kat, to Adrian, to Maria.

Let's open a packet of Twistees, and pour them into a bowl. On the back of the packet it says: 'I have [...] been blessed by the very good fortune of knowing Maria Grech Ganado who very lovingly accepts to translate my work and that of others of my generation.' – Immanuel Mifsud

Fire Alarm Drill

Don't worry, it's just a test! But if you ever hear the fire alarm in future... this is your chance!

It might mean that someone is talking about an author you'd really like to translate, so you have to drop everything and run over to speak with the rights agent, the publisher looking for a translator, the author, all of them, and tell them how much this book means to you, that you have to translate it, please, you're the best person for the job. Go on, get to it!

Once, at a book fair, a translation funder told me the rights had been sold for Michelle Steinbeck's novel, which I had been mesmerised by, so I immediately emailed the publisher who had won the rights, made an appointment ASAP, went to pitch myself to five people sitting opposite me in a basement office, made my case for why I should translate it. It worked.

Or a publisher emails you and asks you to try out for a translation by translating the attached text, ASAP! You prioritise it, even over the book translation you're currently working on, because you need to line up your next job. You might get it; most often you're one of two, three, four, five translators, so the likelihood of not getting it can be high.

Or maybe a magazine asks if you have any translations to publish. You quickly ask around for permission, work all day, all evening, all weekend on a translation, you want people to read this author, and then the magazine might accept it or reject it.

Other times, no alarm goes off, and you won't know that anything is happening at all.

W25 – Karaoke Booth

I hope you all have your karaoke songs at the ready! Everybody into the soundproofed room, I can reassure you there will be no strobing, does anyone want to duet with me?

I found my confidence, and my sense of self, when I started singing as a child. I remember when I was nine or ten, my middle school did a musical about Hades and Persephone. We all had to learn these catchy songs, and I became as obsessed with them as I was with watching *Top of the Pops*, where I would jump up and down and sing right in front of the screen.

My form teacher was the conductor for the musical, and, though I was very scared of her, I went up to her at the end of class one day and asked if I could borrow the cassette of songs. She seemed annoyed by the question – didn't I realise it was the only copy the school had? She allowed me to borrow it for one night. I took the portable stereo from the kitchen windowsill in my house, put it on the landing, played the tape while dancing and singing along.

This led to me going to an amateur dramatics group in my early teens, where, to my parents' and my own dismay, I would be given main roles in each musical because, it turned out, I could sing. Later came singing in D.I.Y. bands, singing on other bands' records. Singing with friends at karaoke bars.

Singing is the one thing I'm sure I can do, and it made me sure of my voice and my control of it. Singing feels like magic.

In writing, we often hear you have to find your voice. And in translation?

I view all of these finding-your-voices as when you stop mimicking and appreciate and embrace what you specifically sound like, your version of someone else's song.

Karaoke is a metaphor, but it's also a networking event.

On the first day I arrived on a residency in Zurich to write a novel, my friend Ulrike, a Swiss German author whom I've never translated but with whom I collaborated on a long original poem, received a literary prize. She organised a karaoke party in a bar to celebrate, and the judges in their suits and smart dresses sat stiffly and watched everyone singing.

I didn't know anyone, but I wanted to start my residency with a bang so I wouldn't immediately revert to my usual standoffish awkwardness. I got up in front of the collective of writers and important stakeholders, as I had done at receptions at London Book Fairs and at embassies to make speeches and thank people, but this time I sang 'Mother' by Danzig – a raunchy rock number by the former frontman of the Misfits.

After I finished, a woman came up to me and said that she had loved my performance. This is how I met Melanie Katz, a German poet based in Zurich. After impressing her with my karaoke performance, we met for coffees, and she invited me for fondue at her house. We kept in touch when I returned to the UK, and when a magazine asked if I had any translations available, I translated some of her poems.

She has just finished translating my poetry collection into German, having found a publisher herself, and is doing so on the side of her job at a university. This is how translation can happen – someone coming up to you after you sing Danzig at karaoke.

I played drums in a few bands, including, for a short time, a Ramones covers band. Which did I like more: playing my own music or playing in a covers band? Singing my own songs, or singing songs at karaoke? I love doing both of them the same. It's drumming, it's singing. Playing in a Ramones covers band made me drum differently, it made me have to improve to meet the Ramones where they were, and once I'd done that, my drumming was better, more versatile. I, too, could write songs that needed the drums to have the qualities of Tommy Ramone.

Often at karaoke with friends, I'll do Elton John. He went viral in lockdown when he performed from his garden. People commented online that instead of singing 'I'm still standing', he was really saying something closer to 'I'm dill danding'. The reason I can see for this is that a) when you're playing to stadiums, *ddd* probably cuts through to the back rows better than *sss*, and b) *ssstillsssstanding* isn't nice to listen to. Margaret Atwood talks in her online MasterClass course about Robert Graves's 'getting the geese out' – removing *sss* sounds from his poetry. In translation, alliteration and hard-to-say phrasings happen unintentionally because we're using new words that need to be tested against one another. A word or two might need to be changed so the sentence doesn't suddenly sound ridiculous, or because you try reading it aloud – something translators often have to do – only to find you trip over the words. Sound is important in all translations, especially poetry. And sometimes the difference between a good translation and a compelling translation is choosing the words that convey the message while making them *sing*.

You have to weigh up all the options to find the one that holds as many of the qualities of the original as possible – meaning, sound, connotation, register, inference... Robert Glück has said: 'Writing is choosing one word over another. Of course, everybody knows that, but sometimes they don't know that.' Sounds a lot like something Milhouse Van Houten says in *The Simpsons* about how difficult it is to write poetry: 'Well, I used a rhyming dictionary, but it only gives you options. The job of the poet is to say, "This one, I guess."'

I can still remember the most satisfying solution I've ever found in translation to match alliteration in the original without losing any of the meaning:

fuzzy physiognomies

I remember it because when I wrote it, I thought to myself: *I'm really doing my job.* It was an extra bonus when the editor, who couldn't read German, highlighted these two words because they loved them together, I'd made them *zing*. Now let's sing!

P509 – A Panel Discussion with Actors and Musicians on Translation

Jeremy Strong, *on attempting and approaching a translation*

'A performance is not a monolith, it's a thousand imperfect attempts at a scene or a moment, and I find, personally, that I feel sort of always on the frontier of uncertainty and confusion. And from that place, making attempts based on your intuition in terms of charting it. I feel very fortunate to be working with material, you know… the writers are so brilliant… so a lot of that needle is threaded for you and like very powerful magnets just sort of pulls out of you what it needs to. And the hardest part is you have to make yourself available to that and be a vessel for it… I have to earn the right to say those words.'

Michelle Williams, *on the chase for the next translation project*

'It's nice to live in that passionate state, that thing where you're so full of desire that burns you to the point where you have to go outside of your comfort zone and make yourself so incredibly vulnerable in front of a stranger and say, "I want this with my whole heart." It's like, such a generative place to live. I'm in a flame right now for this thing, and I don't know if it's going to be expanded or extinguished. But it's such a beautiful place to create from, too. And even if you don't get it, it gets a little bit stronger and stronger and it carries over to the next thing. I kind of love being in a desirous state, like before you consummate something. I think that's actually the most exciting time. This thing exists, and whether I get to touch it or not, it's out there and I'm just grateful to know it's in the universe.'

Colin Farrell, *on loving or not loving your translation projects*

'Sometimes you read scripts and you don't connect in any way, but sometimes you need money and you go and do them anyway. That's happened a couple of times, you know, and even then I'm very grateful to be... like, the majority of people in the world, or a lot of people, I would imagine, don't have a job that they feel connected to.'

Claire Foy, *on translator working conditions and changing expectations*

'I noticed that when I first started acting, I was like, Ooo, this takes up a lot of time, and a lot of my life, and I'm expected to give a lot of my life over, and even then I thought, I don't think that's actually OK. And now what I've noticed is, I've just started to not think that I have to do anyone a favour. Like, I'm being employed to do a job, you're paying me, I'm here, I'm committed, I want to do this, this is great, but because an industry is creative, sometimes there is an idea that it doesn't have to be professional... There are boundaries to be respected; I think it's OK to say, "We're going to work till 8 p.m. and then we stop."'

Sharon Stone, *on mutual respect and harmony between author and translator*

'[They] did not ask for anything from me – just asked me if I would do it and trusted me. We just innately understand each other, at an almost intimate level. We have no judgment of each other; we have only affirmative feelings about each other as an artist. It's not a competitive sport, but we want each other to bring our best game, and in order to do that, it's like, "Just go for it, girl."'

Jeremy Strong, quoting Edvard Munch, *on how translation is literature*

'Painting must not merely reconstruct a moment, it must itself be a moment.'

Tracee Ellis Ross, *on translation as embodied; translation as play, experimentation, imagination*

'I said "there's a man on the roof and he's going to jump" three different ways... and I was like, if this is what acting is, where I get to use my imagination, everything about myself, I get to act from my full body, I'm in, I'm sold.'

Colin Farrell, *on bringing your mood and your self to your translation*

'I didn't have any fear that Colin could be seen through [the pros-thetics]. You know some days you wake up as an actor and you're having a shit day, man. Like people do. You've had bad dreams, some-thing's not going right in your personal life, you go into work and you have to pretend to be someone else. That could sound like a relief – oh well, you're having a shit time as yourself, so cool, you get a few hours to be someone else. Not really! You can't not bring yourself to the party. You're always there.'

Dave Grohl, *on why two translations of the same text will be different*

'If you get two drummers to play the same piece of sheet music it will sound different because of life, heart, soul.'

Josh Brolin, *on translating more than one project at the same time*

'It was an incredible four years of my life where I would do two plays in rotating rep and sometimes do a classic piece, but I was always doing two plays at once, which was – which might seem to be – confusing, but which was actually a really great skill to be able to pop in and out of something, or do one thing in the afternoon and go and do a completely different character at night.'

Salma Hayek, *on translation as bringing your perspective on a story*

'Producing is hell, writing is frustrating, acting is really satisfying, directing is heaven. [...] I think for me, the draw would be that sometimes I have a story to tell, and I don't want the limitation of my body and who I am to tell just one character of someone else's story, but to tell the perspective of a story that you have a special perspective on. Like, if your brain is wired in a way that the way you can tell it is not so much with words but with moods and the little moments, the details, you know, you want to feel it, feel the light, be able to put the music into it... I think it's a way of being wired, having that perspective.'

Lizzo, *on composing a translation*

'Being classically trained is incredible because I feel like I can speak a language... You hear the track and you think, Damn, this is a rich piece of music... It's understanding the time signature, you're in harmony, and dissonance and rhythm and cadence.'

Brian Cranston, *on how translation isn't a one-off, it's a lifetime*

'That is what a real love of acting is, it's a relationship, it's not a fling, it is committing to something for the rest of your life. When I think of creating and writing and acting it occupies all of me, and I love it. If I ever start to complain about going to work at six o'clock in the morning...'

Daniel Kaluuya, *on 'accessible excellence' as a translation approach*

'The goal of making films for the friends you grew up with... As an actor, how do you think about the balance between a film's high-minded thesis and then just the basic North Star of entertaining people first and foremost? [...] It's like... was it Bob Marley? You want to say something so a baby can understand it. I think it's a symptom of understanding if you say it simply. So that's my thing, it's like, it's all good knowing all this stuff, but can you translate it?'

Rice Pudding Stand

A banner over the stand: 'Barbot completely opened my eyes to personal interpretation. At the time, I did everything by the book. I didn't feel ready to have my own interpretation.' – Chef Adeline Grattard, *Chef's Table: France*

Written on the napkins at the stand is a quote from Mary Berry: 'I've written hundreds of recipes and people get different results dependent on the temperature of the oven or their technique.' – Episode 1, Series 1, *The Great British Bake Off*

Writer and avid cook Rebecca May Johnson – who was a PhD student studying German poetry translation when I met her during my postgrad – has a rice pudding stand at the Fair. She is partly recreating a performance I commissioned her to do for the closing event of the exhibition I'd curated at the Austrian cultural centre 'Translation as Firework'. At the exhibition, I'd invited friends who were ceramicists, tattooists, makers, musicians, filmmakers, photographers to translate my translation of a short story by Austrian writer Anna Weidenholzer into their mediums.

Rebecca wrote a recipe laying out the cross-cultural powers of rice pudding, or Milchreis:

> When thinking about what recipe I want to come up with, I always imagine how I want the resulting eating to make me feel. [...] These feelings, along with specific elements of context – Germanness, Turkishness – were what I tried to convey through my translation of the story into a recipe. I think our bodies can be better diplomats and translators than our minds, realising and becoming fluent in the joy of difference, long before we are intellectually ready to engage in it.

Rebecca cooked two dishes for the guests' enjoyment, but also so that they, the audience, could in turn translate their eating experience into text. She asked those in the audience to write down what the recipe made them feel, think, remember. This resulted in crafted poems, childhood memories, witty ditties and wondrous fragments. She had translated the recipe from text into food, and the audience translated the food in an act of eating into their own personal experience of it.

Years later, Rebecca asked me, along with a few other writers, to cook a rice pudding recipe and write down the experience. I noted:

> Soya milk's already sweetened, so I only used half the required sugar. (It's like when I'm translating a piece of German literature and I have to do some rebalancing – if the translated text is already turning out pretty sweet in the process, you might downplay the natural sweetness elsewhere to avoid oversweetness. We might also alter a recipe, like a translation, due to ethics and tastes, consciously or unconsciously. Cooking a written recipe is always translation, it needs interpreting.)

Canteen

Rebecca also wrote a very popular essay about canteens, so she set this up for us here. It's the food I used to get in the canteen when I worked in an office in Munich. Cheap, filling, wholesome food, not overpriced sandwiches.

My mum went to catering college. When we were children she sometimes liked to bake, using a recipe or making things from memory. In his retirement, my dad became my mum's full-time carer and got into baking, mainly bread and different cakes like Bakewell tarts and Belgian buns. My dad often made things my mum used to make before she became too unwell.

When I used to visit and I asked what they'd been up to that day, he'd say, 'We've been making Mum's profiteroles.' This actually meant that my dad had been making profiteroles while my mum sat in her armchair, or was in bed. What he was saying is: *I've been making profiteroles, like your mum used to make, to the recipe and in the way she used to make them.*

Though he'd made them many times, he still asked for her advice about the way to proceed. He'd ask her questions from the kitchen. He'd ask what she made of them: *She thought they were pretty good*. He recognised that it was her tradition, art and expertise, and though he was carrying it on, it belonged to her, or it was theirs together.

Coffee Break

You find yourself now on this miraculously large indoor piazza covered with assorted tables and chairs – all the meetings I've had with editors and other translators and event programmers and writers I've translated, and the moment I said out loud for the first time that I wanted to be a literary translator to my friend Martha over a beer, take place here, over and over again, in a looped performance by actors wearing wigs and costumes. I won't be entering with you this time, I'll wait here.

On the left, you'll see a man in his early forties. Clean and well kempt, sitting up very straight at a table. This is Gregor Hens, the first German author, probably the first author at all, I ever met for coffee. I'm in my mid-twenties, I quit my job at the German cultural centre to be a full-time translator and writer the year before.

It was like meeting a character in a book, because he *was* a character in a book. I was translating his memoir. I tried to seem grown up; I was incredibly nervous. Meeting strangers in coffee shops, older men I didn't know, famous ones who were full-time authors, was still something very new to me.

Order a coffee from the counter, you're shaking. Join this author at his table. See, he's smiling very gently. The napkins and the cups and the saucers are monogrammed with his initials – G. H. He talks to you about his life and asks you about yours, as if a mutual friend had recommended you meet him. He tells you that he wants you to do what you have to do. He understands. He's a translator too, a very established one. He tells you that he lost a lot of weight from stress while translating a famously verbose English writer. You feel very comfortable with him. You sense he trusts you, though he has no reason to. His English is better than your English, but you know he'll only try once or twice to suggest alternative words or lines. On a plate are etched the words Anthea Bell wrote about translating Sebald: 'Some authors ask a translator why a certain phrase can't be used in

English, as if the translator were to blame, but not Max; he knew that language develops of its own accord.' You've never translated a book for adults before, and you're going to have to write about his addiction, his father's anger, his mother's death. You shuffle how you imagined the scenes from the book to look in your mind. But now, having talked with him, you see them in a more amusing, absurd, darkly comic light. You can now hear his deadpan tone when you read the book; can you hear his voice reading it in your headset? You leave the coffee feeling like he's your peer. You feel like you've joined a special club. You feel like a literary translator.

Let's go back a year. On the corner of the piazza, over there, a bit in the distance, we've set up a propped-up facade of a chain café. A few of you can go behind it, climb up a ladder and peer down on the scene from the window. The ground is wet from a rainstorm – oh, sorry, can someone throw this bucket of water on the floor? The sun is just coming out – lights! – the weather is nice enough now for a few people to sit outside. Can you see, opposite the café on the piazza, an image of the entrance leading to the underground station has been projected onto the wall? You've not come from the station. You've come from the office you work at, it's around midday. The person you're meeting seems to be sitting at one of the tables.

Don't be alarmed by the lights turning red. Or maybe you should be.

This translator you're meeting is over twice your age and in translation circles, as well as in your imagination and in the place where your future ambitions lie dormant. You are no one in this world, you are only a young editor going to interview them. The receptionist at the French cultural centre around the corner reminds you of how she announced your arrival on the telecom at your first out-of-house meeting two years ago at the German cultural centre, by shouting it across the silent piazza: *La jeune fille, elle est là* – the young girl is here. Or you could say 'the young lass', or 'the maiden', even.

You must concentrate on looking older than twenty-four as you walk towards the café. Make your approach. I need you to focus, I need you to take it all in and report back for me, everyone. Get closer and say his name, any name will do, he will still stand up regardless, put out your hand to shake, feel energised and relieved to be entering an honourable and memorable moment in your pre-translation career, he takes your hand and uses it against you, he pulls you towards him very quickly, and purposefully kisses you half – which is actually more like sixty to seventy per cent, but half sounds neater – on your unfamiliar and noncompliant mouth, knowing that you will have no option but to pretend he kissed you on the cheek. It's purposeful because – did you see? – he redirects and darts his puckered lips towards yours. Did you see it? I wish I could slow it down for you, but I can't show it again, not straight away, not for a while. It's started a tone ringing in our ears, can you hear it? Has your body stiffened? Go into the shop and get a coffee. Sit down with him. You can't really speak. He talks at you erratically. Let him talk. He asks you personal questions about your relationships. He says something disparaging about how women can't translate as well as men. The rest sounds like nothing but noise. At the end, move the both of you into a more open space to say goodbye, being in the middle of a busy street might make things advantageous for you. Thank him and offer your hand for him to shake. Did you put your hand out the first time? You certainly have the second time. He grips it, he pulls, his lips dart, he kisses you fully on the mouth, he walks away without a goodbye. You stand there in the street, strangely alone and vulnerable even though the street is crowded and you never feel vulnerable. You can't move from where you're standing for a few minutes.

A purple neon sign overwriting the café's name switches on. It reads:

But I told him I wanted to be a translator?

Snack Stand

Chips! Pommes!

When I translated an excerpt from Ilija Matusko's memoir, it was one of the only times I had translated a book by someone who, like myself, had grown up in a working-class, non-arts household before going into writing. The memoir talks about going to school smelling of chip fat from his parents' restaurant, how people could smell the working-classness on him. I remember the smell of oil my dad would bring in from fixing cars, the smell of chicken fat on me from working on a deli counter in a supermarket.

Before I learnt German, I learnt how to pass as middle class. 'You sound well posh,' my mum told me once when I was young. I must have picked up how my teachers spoke, or maybe accents from the TV.

Katy Derbyshire writes in her essay 'Mother Tongue / Muttersprache' about her mum's English being 'an acquired language' after time spent at boarding school. I used to be proud of being able to put on being 'well spoken', but now I let my mouth do the talking.

I was asked to speak from a working-class perspective on a translation panel and someone joked beforehand, *are you going to wear a tracksuit?* Presumably they wondered if I would *read* as working class. I didn't wear one, though I'm wearing one now. I was told at a party thrown by a publisher I've translated for not to keep mentioning that I'd bought my dress in a charity shop. I suppose it spoiled the illusion.

My accent and how I present reveal that I'm not actually middle-class, and not actually German. A friend asked me to speak German, and I said a few bits, and they said I should put on a thicker German accent. That felt wrong to me, because I'm an English person speaking another language, it would feel like telling my dad to put on a thicker English accent (like Katy Derbyshire and her mother, I also don't think my dad has an accent, but others tell me otherwise).

My background allows me to code-switch, a great muscle to strengthen for translation, its own form of code-switching, not just between Englishes but between a bunch of German codes and a range of English codes.

The first time I spoke at the London Book Fair many years ago, I felt like I had made it as a literary translator. The most recent time, I travelled to the fair to speak on a panel so I could announce to the room that I was busier than ever but that I only had about thirty pounds left in my account because every publisher, institution and organisation I'd done translations or translation teaching for was behind on paying me, and I have no safety net. Out of the frying pan of grifting, into the fire of contempt.

Yes, I have a chip on my shoulder.

Cash Point

If you need a top-up, you'll find the cash point to the left, next to the money trees. The amusing thing with flashing coloured lights around it.

I remember building myself up to reply to a publisher who had tried to haggle down my fee during the month of December after I had minimally raised it after ten years of doing translation work for them, and when I finally sent it, I got an out of office. *I'm on my winter break till mid-January*. A paid holiday I'll never have. It's the same for free-lance editors, journalists, writers, art workers, musicians – those situated outside employment, producing skilled work and being paid far less than they should be, less by the year.

Andy Hodges, a fiction editor, said in an interview: 'The "translation as art" paradigm sometimes pops up, and it irks me. It can easily lead to self-exploitation and isn't practical outside of an academic world of grants, stipends and prizes.'

I would argue that a) literary translation *is* analogous to art – a creative practice like writing (I would know, I am a writer, musician, maker), and b) I would not say I am exploiting myself, it is others who exploit me. There is nothing shameful about naming oneself a victim.

Calling oneself an artist is not what leads to the exploitation of artists, it's the culture industry that exploits artists, and institutions and governments that teach people to undervalue them as skilled, expert workers. The previous government said that they wanted to get rid of degrees that go on to support 'low-paying' jobs. My job is low-paying, but it's not because of my degrees, it's because of large, profit-hoarding publishers and a societal devaluing of the arts.

One thing's for certain: no matter how much I work, no matter how steady my translation commissions, no matter the accolades and respect I garner, I cannot earn enough money to sustain myself and this job. (I awoke one morning from no dreams feeling like I had become an abject failure.)

Some people, including other kinds of translators, say, *well just stop, then!*

Up to now, I have refused to stop.

If we all stopped doing what was underfunded and underpaid, it would be what I call the triple punishment in comparison to the single punishment – I don't get to do the thing I love and am good at; it will happen less or will simply stop happening; *and* I'll go from not getting paid much to getting paid nothing. What if it's all I can do, what I've been training for years to do? What if it's the thing that makes me feel like a complete human being? I translate. But I'm being put in a difficult position.

It's not about being entitled to work – no one, including in creative jobs, is entitled to a job, not currently anyway. It's about being paid fairly for work you have been commissioned to do. I don't want or expect to become wealthy. I'd be happy with large publishers paying a lot more, smaller publishers paying the same or less or even in some cases not much, depending on the project. When a one-person publisher commissioned a translation of mine, she split the profits equally between herself, me and the designer, because she was so happy with our work, she knew we had worked long hours and late nights and weekends to make it happen, and she wanted to acknowledge that the book was all of ours. It's the only time I've ever been given a bonus for a translation.

There's another way of looking at this. Instead of a publisher *passively* underpaying me and not giving me even a one per cent royalty, they are *actively* asking me to invest in their company (the rest of my fee and the royalty stays with them) and to share in the burden of the risk of the book (instead of paying me properly and taking on the risk of the book themselves – they commissioned it, after all). I'm not willing to invest in someone that doesn't seem invested in me.

Thank you for paying for your ticket to the Fair.

Sinkhole!

Watch out! Sinkholes have been opening up all over the Fair, and beyond its walls. Three sinkholes are currently dotted around Hastings; more open up when the town floods biannually/annually/half-yearly (it's getting worse).

At first, we cordoned off the ones in the Fair with red-and-white cones and tape. Then I had an idea.

I had translated a novel, *Das flüssige Land*, *The Liquid Land*, by the Austrian author Raphaela Edelbauer, which is about a fictional village/town/city (it's fluid in the book) called Greater Einland. The whole place is falling into a sinkhole, but everyone carries on like nothing is happening and discards things they want to forget into the hole. Within a couple of years of one another, the English writer Rosanna Mclaughlin and Raphaela Edelbauer both wrote novels about sinkholes and national identity; both are brilliant, both show that images and issues cross borders at times simultaneously.

The head of Greater Einland (it was actually called Gross-Einland, which could have been Great Einland, but that sounded too much like Great Britain, and I liked how the connotation of Greater made it feel more competitive) wants to turn it into a tourist attraction. I thought this was a great idea, so I've put up a permanent railing you can get through for a fee, and a little ladder you can go down so you can wander through my buried self.

You might find:

a grainy photo of me being spat on by a German man on an empty street while living in Munich because he thought I was a Turkish immigrant, 'Türken raus!'

a looping gif playing in a puddle of the moment someone told me that I didn't *look like* I would translate German, and that it would *make more sense* if I translated Maltese a clump of sticky knowledge that I'll never really be fluent in German, be good enough in Maltese to converse with my relatives, or know every word or turn of phrase in English.

Signing Table!

At this row of tables near T4, filled with brand new pens of all varieties, your favourite translators will manifest before you to talk about and sign their translations.

You can talk to them for as long as you like – ask them questions, quote your favourite lines, give them gifts, get your photo taken with them.

Most of these translators have not written their own work, but they are some of the best writers we have. Let's shower them with appreciation.

I'm allowed to jump the queue!

Who will you summon to the tables? Write a list of their names below.

Via L14 – Tunnel of Love

All of you choose an animal boat and climb in.

My little swan boat bobs and rocks. Before it floats off into the tunnel's darkness, its chipped paint is visible, this white swan's previous pink, blue and yellow lives can be seen underneath this latest layer, and its eyes look bulbous and spooked. The mouth of the tunnel seems to suck the little boat into its hot darkness, which has the sharp reek of chlorine.

After a few moments of imperceptibly drifting, time measured by dripping, the first fake lantern with a pink heart-shaped plastic flame appears on the tunnel wall.

Someone has appeared in the seat beside me – one of the authors I translated. They have their head turned away from me. They sent me numerous emails wanting me to send them the translation early while I was working on it, and then once they had it they ghosted me, never to get in touch again, my congratulatory messages on publication day ignored.

Darkness again. I sense movement next to me.

I look and see another of my authors, they smile at me and hand me a copy of their latest book, and ask after me and my partner.

In the next period of darkness I feel a hand on my thigh; passing into the light, I see an author whose short story I translated for a magazine. He smiles at me suggestively. I push him out of the boat.

As the boat rights itself in the pitch black, I feel it weighed down beside me again. The next lantern appears from around the corner.

Taking his place is a furtive-looking author who wanted me to translate his poetry. He came to watch my band play but didn't come and say hello, informing me afterwards that he had been watching me.

He sent me repeated emails to translate his work, each more aggressive than the last.

The dark. An author I like a lot, who gently said via email, 'I don't need to see that' when I showed them my first, messy draft, like I'd flashed them or shown them an unhealed wound, passes me a coffee.

Now beside me sits an author whose book was shortlisted for a major prize, and then again in my translation. In their citation for the prize, the judges said that the book was an example of where translation is like a dance, and that we seemed to be equal dance partners. They said that they could tell how closely we had collaborated on the book because of the quality of the translation. These comments felt alienating to me when put in contrast with the reality of our relationship. I felt fraudulent, I doubted my translation for a moment – could I have produced such a great translation if in fact we had had no contact during the process, just a couple of polite emails at the end where I asked a few questions?

Darkness. I feel cold. Then a big grin like the Cheshire Cat starts glowing in the darkness... It's Michelle Steinbeck!

She tells me in a rush where she is in the world, holding my hand.

The last time I saw her we spent a long weekend together in Paris where we lied to each other and the wider world that we were going to be working on translations of her short stories, and instead drank coffee and wine, smoked cigarettes, ate ice cream, took walks, took naps. We shared her studio apartment, where she was on another residency. It was strictly forbidden for her to have guests, so we had to wait for the receptionist to walk away so we could make a dash for the lift, snickering, and came back late in the evening to avoid being caught.

We talked late into the night outside a bar about our lives – with Michelle, I never feel like I'm the audience to an award-winning author, I feel like I am talking with a friend. This is because I am. I'm grateful that translation brought me Michelle.

Would you be able to tell that we are close friends from my translations of her work? If I hadn't told you (and I might be lying) that we are close friends, could you see it in my translation? Why am I even telling you we're friends? Maybe because I want you to see that closeness. Maybe I want you to find my translation's authenticity via my friendship with my authors – how could it not be good if we're friends? If we're close friends, so must be our books.

And why does it matter to me that I'm close with my authors, why do I want them to like me and feel close to me? Could I want to pre-empt conflict, or do I want validation (of me, of my work), or to simply gain their trust so I can get on with the translation unimpeded?

If I'm aware deep down that authors, no matter how good their English, are sometimes the last people who can judge whether my translation is good, why do I get a thrill when they pronounce in interviews or at events that they think I did a good job? Whether it's right or not, public sign-off on who I am as a person and of the translation I've produced means it's more likely people will trust my translation – and trust themselves to enjoy it.

Being friends with Michelle doesn't mean that I suddenly know her writing as well as she does, or that she can make my decisions for me. She knows and I know that I'm the translator, and that I have to find the answers in the text itself. Friendship doesn't mean less finesse.

I don't think friendship guarantees a translation will be better or worse, but it can make the collaboration more or less enjoyable, and it can create trust. It means I can try things and not scare an author; it allows me to be my most vulnerable and to show early drafts and ask even more questions – these might make the translation better, or perhaps just different.

One of the greatest side effects of translating for me are the unplanned friendships that happen in the process. In the worst-case scenario, the translation feels like a service to an uncaring client; in the best case, it feels like the useful by-product of a wonderful experience with someone – a meal we cooked together, handed to someone else to enjoy (and critique) so we can have another drink and continue chatting.

Toilets

Anyone need to use the facilities?

Cubicle 1

The first short story I ever wrote and shared with others was plagiarised.

My mum would get given a bunch of women's magazines from our neighbour – *Take a Break, Pick Me Up, Woman's Weekly* – and they would be in a pile on the bathroom floor. I would sometimes flick through them when I was on the toilet, enjoying the closed-off, shut-away atmosphere of the bathroom. On Sundays when life was slower, the bathroom radio would hiss out distorted football chants and measured commentary – translations of action on the pitch – and the washing machine or the dryer would be thrumming rhythmically next to me. There was no rush.

One of the magazines had stories in them, and I liked to read them during these alone times in the downstairs loo. These were the only magazines we had, and the only taste of contemporary fiction writing I was exposed to. It felt exciting to read a short story that someone had written very recently and had accepted to a popular magazine.

The stories were written in straightforward, everyday language and reminded me of the first and only book for adults I'd read outside school by that age, Roald Dahl's story collection *Someone Like You*, which I kept by my bed at all times. I had been drawn to it in a charity shop because of its black cover with an eerie, brightly coloured eye staring out of it.

The magazine's stories were domestic and very English and accessible, very different from the very old and/or very American books we were reading at school when I was fifteen.

One day I read a story with a twist I couldn't stop thinking about. In the first part of the story, a hungover and controlling man and his younger partner are in a car accident while driving to visit her parents.

In the second half of the story, the man is distraught and distressed and alone in a clinical place, where we listen to his thoughts about the crash, about the people working on 'her' at that moment. When his partner enters near the end, it becomes apparent that the 'her' and 'she' he had been reminiscing about was in fact his car, and that they are not in a hospital but in a garage. I thought it was really clever, and I read it and reread it to unlock its set-up, characterisation, unveiling of tension, its reveal and its ending. I liked the story so much, I wanted to write it myself.

I started writing my own version, paraphrasing every line and adapting the metaphors to be my own. I saw gaps in the story, entry-ways to add details or expand. I added a pile of art books to the man's bedside table (I had started becoming interested in art after my first visit to an art gallery earlier that year with school) and a bruise on the young woman's leg. While the original ending had come directly after the twist, I had the young woman be picked up by her parents, to leave him for good.

I was so pleased with what I came up with, I gave it in as home-work (not coursework! not marked work!), and the next lesson my teacher announced that I had written an excellent story and that she wanted to read it out for the class. I was mortified, but also thrilled. The rowdier kids, forced to sit at the front, all made annoyed noises, everyone stared at me. My teacher read out the story slowly, mea-suredly, pausing when needed. When the twist came, one of the boys, who was known to go bright red with anger and throw chairs, lifted his head up from his arms in disbelief. When the ending came, every-one clapped. I felt proud.

I didn't feel like I was copying or ripping off someone, I felt like I was learning how a story was put together, that I was engaging with a peer and with a great idea, through the act of doing the writing myself. I had taken the markers and prompts in the original story and had made it my own. I never versioned or copied a story again, not directly or intentionally in any case, but this act gave me the confidence to start writing. The feeling of reading something and rewriting it myself is now a familiar one.

I've always had a reactive, generative writing practice, always writing *after* something else in the wake of it fascinating and exciting me, and giving me a strange confidence to do it myself.

Cubicle 2

Once, during an event with an author I had translated, I snuck off to the toilets to text with one of my other authors to tell them I missed them and that I wished they were here, like someone in a relationship surreptitiously texting an ex.

Plumbing

My creativity is a state that finds an outlet, like water running through pipes until it finds a crack to leak from. Once a hole is plugged, it searches for another place to run. If I'm not careful it could seep into acting, dancing, making. Before, I would often translate two books at the same time, I would be reading two, three, four, five books at the same time. After translating more than one book at the same time, out of no plan of my own, I started writing two novels at the same time. I had been working on one for many years, the other for just over a year, but I finished their full drafts within weeks of each other. This isn't showing off, or humblebragging. It was stressful, almost distressing.

They just came to a head that way, together. It's like a chamber has opened up in my mind from working across two or more translations or my own writing projects, and all the chambers must be filled at all times. Two reading books, two translations, two novels, they don't care, just fill them, feed them! Actually, it was three books, if you count this Fair.

Someone's written some graffiti on the pipes in sharpie: 'this knock-off aqueduct that carries / not the water but the thirst' – Amit Majmudar, 'Translators'

Enter through the fringe curtains into this hut that is actually a vast theatre.

Our first act is... a mind reader!

I can see... nothing at all.

The biggest issue in translation is that we can't read the author's mind to understand why they wrote something the way they did, the steps they took, if they intended for something to be read one way or the other. A translator doesn't know if a line is just a line, or the key to the whole book.

There were a couple of things I was finding really vague in one book I was translating, almost like references to cultural or historical events I didn't know, so I checked them with the author. They told me they were things they'd dreamt or private events they'd experienced in childhood, that I would have had to have been there, they were as self-contained and closed-off as in-jokes. Writers sometimes forget that their writing has to meet the world, has to have context, has to be comprehended in some way, even if that means hinting to the reader that they won't be able to understand the reference. I could never have entered their dreams or entered their childhood – I only have the Internet.

I can see... a table.

I read an academic paper where, in an attempt at a scientific analysis of how a French text changed in English translation, they placed words in the original French text on a spectrum of potential transformation. The word 'table' was designated as a 'neutral' word, that is, it could be translated pretty much directly and wasn't worth measuring.

I instantly thought to myself: but what kind of table are we talking about?

Depending on where it was, a table could become a desk, it could become a dressing table, it could become a dinner table. Even tables have the potential to change in translation because a table transforms depending on where it's placed in an English space.

'My daughter sat at the table in her room.'

If she was sitting to do her homework, I might translate it as 'desk'. If she was looking in a mirror, I might translate it as 'dressing table'. Table, in English, is a general word. If there's a bunch of them in the room: *Can you stack those tables?* If there's only one table in the room: *It's over there on the table.* Ultimately, as long as the reader pictures a table, the job's done.

Is this the table you were picturing?

Next up, we have a performance of the dramatic monologue *Not I* by Samuel Beckett, acted by Jess Thom, aka Touretteshero.

Thom had to get special permission from the Beckett Estate to perform the piece because the estate stipulates that absolutely nothing can be changed or added or taken away from a piece by Beckett in performance.

As Thom has Tourette's syndrome, this would not be possible. When you watch Thom's performance, there are interjections, including a common tic she says, which is 'biscuit'.

Would you want a translator adding something to a translation? Would you want someone who is not a perfect speller translating literature? Someone who uses a different kind of English to you? Even if it had all the feeling, all the meaning, even if that voice actually enhanced the book? A review in the *New York Times* of Thom's *Not I* called her 'an ideal interpreter':

Who would know better what it means to live, as Mouth does, between silence and uncontrolled speech? Who would know better what it feels like to have a 'mouth on fire' and 'something begging in the brain,' than someone with Tourette's? In her genial welcome to the performance, which is also signed for the deaf and 'relaxed' for those on the autism spectrum, Thom says that in working on the play she came to feel that Beckett was writing about a woman like herself.

Sometimes I translate in order to write about myself. In almost every book I've translated I've found a part of myself and have used this to my/the translation's advantage.

By the way, I make grammatical and spelling errors all the time. Sophie Hughes often lovingly recalls my confession that I don't know the difference between *past* and *passed*. I still don't, I can't figure it out. But this is partly what editors are for – to allow me to do the bulk of the job, and to support me.

My favourite writer on my creative writing module at university was someone who hadn't grown up in the UK and who had come to the UK to study, whose stories were the most well written, well crafted. All our tutor could say about their writing was that their English wasn't perfect.

The actress Ana de Armas was criticised for portraying Marilyn Monroe with a slight Cuban accent. Her accent.

Robin Munby has written about translating into scouse dialect, something he learnt growing up in Liverpool, and how to translate is not to create a product under capitalism, but to speak in response to someone who has spoken.

Deborah Smith has said that she used regional Yorkshire words in her translations of Han Kang. Her words.

The Scottish actor Jack Lowden from *Slow Horses* has talked about how he likes acting with his own accent because he can tap into his creativity a lot quicker.

The literary critic John Self recently wrote online: 'Reading a novel which is translated by a Scots translator and uses the verb "swithered", making it suddenly seem like the narrator is not from Denmark but from Dundee.' I mean, the narrator doesn't speak English at all, why do they have to speak fantasy-placeless English?

Brian Robert Moore, a Northern Irish translator, writes:

> I wish that translations were not so wary of regionalisms in general. None of us have this kind of neutral, standard English – that doesn't exist. Writers can draw on everything, and try to make the richest, most complex works from a linguistic perspective – I wish that there was not such a fear of a similar technique in translation. There are a lot of reasons why people are sceptical of doing things like that, but being narrow-minded about it never helps. There needs to be more conversations about it.

Let's speak lots of voices in our own voices.

Why should I put on a voice? Why must all literature be homogenously written or translated into middle-class (southern) British/US English? It's not neutral, it's a choice.

I actually want you to hear me in my translation, because I can't change my being there. A good translator, I would say, is someone who puts all of who they are into their rendering.

I would read any translation smattered with crumbs and covered in fingerprints.

024 – Haunted House

This stand is done up like a haunted translation house. Don't be scared, they're just translators! I know, I know, they're usually invisible and you don't like to think of those spooks being real...

Literary translators are a lot like ghostwriters. Where a ghostwriter translates interviews into a prose narrative, I turn German literature into English literature. The ghostliness is similar – no one wants to know about this supernatural medium. Ghostwriter Barbara Feinman Todd's memoir is called *Pretend I'm Not Here*. That could be the title of a translator's memoir. It's not just in the idea that we are writing someone else's book that we're similar, it's also the lack of recognition (no names on the cover, no involvement in promotion) and the isolation of ghostwriters from one another. Liam Pieper writes of ghostwriting celebrity memoirs:

> It's all very discreet. I don't know why. Maybe it's a publisher initiative to stop ghost writers meeting and unionising. Perhaps it's because some folks are sniffy about ghost-writing, as though it's somehow unseemly or immoral. Which is silly. Ghost-writing is the most morally sound thing I will do on any given day.
> [...]
> More likely to kill me [than the client] is my workload, and the whiplash of forming and ending so many intense relationships so fast. It's something I'm working through with my therapist – who has a job much like mine but is smart enough to make more money from it.

Translators sometimes say that they are 'channelling' their author, or that they feel 'possessed' by them – usually when the author in question is dead, though not always. Lauren Elkin felt like she was in Simone de Beauvoir's body as she translated a long-lost novel by her; Katrina Dodson and Idra Novey felt possessed and haunted by Clarice Lispector; Jennifer Croft felt like she was inside Olga Tokarczuk's brain!

Michael Hofmann prefers his authors dead: they can't answer back. I can't relate. I want to talk to my author, and also, I'm just not them – I don't embody them, they're not controlling my typing like when fingers drift a glass across a Ouija board. I want a collaborator, but also, I'm not building them like some Frankenstein's monster, re-animating them, I'm rebuilding a text.

If I'm possessed by anyone, it's the characters and the text as it appears as a voice in my head. I don't serve my authors like Igor, I don't want to be them, I have to get to know them and then be wholly myself. If anything I'm like Dracula, absorbing their skills with every bite. And being Dracula sounds more sexy than being possessed. (One of the books I'm translating right now includes a possession, incidentally – a character possessed by another character, written by an author and translated by me.)

There are those who think that translations should be dry, matter of fact, using the most basic vocabulary. This, for me, is translation as autopsy report, rather than as something living that can go out into the world. Emily Wilson wrote online about a message from a reader of her *Odyssey* translation: 'I first read the poem many decades ago in high school, and was clueless. I've tried several times since, but could never get close to it, until now. You've made the book alive for me.'

It's alive!

Flies/CCTV

You might notice flies everywhere on the walls, big fat juicy ones, like the fly on a giant soft-serve ice-cream next to a fly-like surveillance drone on top of Heather Phillipson's Fourth Plinth sculpture 'THE END'. These flies are actually our CCTV, watching and recording everything.

If you get close enough to one of them, you'll see the German filmmaker Werner Herzog reflected in multiple in their eyes, and they'll speak like him, but high-pitched and buzzy:

> The idea of cinéma vérité is a historical mistake. We are not going to withdraw ourselves. We are creators. We are film-makers. We are directors, dammit! Otherwise the surveillance camera in the bank would be the greatest of all cameras. But you can wait for 15 years and not a single bank robbery is going to happen. So it's not what I want and that's not what we are made for as film-makers: go out, shape a film, articulate it, stylise it, use music, use your sense of storytelling. Be active, don't sit back like a fly on the wall. That's idiotic.

Though Herzog got me into German cinema and culture in its early stages, there is no denying his exploitation of people in the creation of his art. I am charmed by him and his Germanness, but he breaks all my rules. More and more, Germany breaks all my rules in its censorship and violence against its own people, its warping of history for present-day gains. I don't know if I find it so charming anymore, I'm not sure I want to be the sprinkles on its soft/sweetly soft-serve power any longer. A fellow literary translator from German recently stated that translating German-language literature was comparatively unpolitical – I don't think this could be further from the truth.

I zoom in on translation-washing. I zoom in on how I've never been commissioned to translate an author who is of mixed heritage and/ or not white. I zoom in on the kinds of texts I could be translating.

Here are some fly swatters. Go to town.

The Floor

If you look down, you'll see a crack zig-zagging across the floor of the Fair. We've painted lines from the drafts of the poet-translator <u>Michael Hamburger</u> onto the floor where he made corrections – either side of the crack, you can see the word in the first draft, and the subsequent change.

Michael changes his mind

Last game of boules in the lamplight   camplight
it's time for my mighty   nightly disappearing act
the convent disappears up in the blue   dissolved in blueness
the garden's history and the city's are not of interest   don't interlock
patriotic doubt   political uncertainty
in the garden of stars   the starry garden
when he gulped down those mouthpieces   those mouthings
disapproval of social peasants   parasites like myself
to keep at evening   at nightfall
sleep and death, the dusky   the dark
smell of lost moss   lost moors
a disarming twinkle of mixed   innocent roguery in his eyes
look, a timid boat is sinking   a timorous boat goes down
the shed blood gathers moon coolness   lunar coolness
if your friends you forget   if you drop an old friend
you watchful powers   you powerful fates
wild ones before you rightly   or   more justly languish
as without light he withered   he writhed
dark and little   dark and lithe
on roses   of roses
heterosexual   homosexual
bicycles roll lonely   slowly
in the evening's depth the blue source's   the wellspring's
for good are statues   are statutes
wittingly   unwittingly
I should scream   scram
in haste and piety   or   haste and pity
yet I did misjudge you   yet I did not misjudge you

When I was translator-in-residence at the British Library, I took the opportunity to have a look at the uncatalogued archive of Hamburger on a casual basis over the course of six months. He's a translator I admire – his translations of the poet <u>Hans Magnus Enzensberger</u> stood out for me in an anthology of Enzensberger's poetry – and I wanted to see the traces of his own translating process, clues as to the practice of a master translator from German into English.

One way of revealing the uniqueness and humanness – the inevitable fallibility – of a translator is through their habits and idiosyncrasies. As I started leafing through Hamburger's drafts and correspondences ('Allow me one day to tell you how badly paid it is to be a translator'), I got to witness where he had handwritten on his typewritten manu-scripts a new way of translating a line or a word, even corrections to whole lines that had been translated incorrectly, and I saw his own corrected spelling mistakes. There were patterns. On multiple occas-ions he had written 'mean' instead of 'men', 'sourthern' rather than 'southern', and there were some great clangers that would have been devastating – or maybe not even noticed – had they made it to print. I started collecting them.

The chances of these mistakes making it through would have been cut down dramatically by the entrance of one of the many great editors who had commissioned and edited his work. I was admitted-ly getting to see him at the vulnerable stage of a translation, when it's just a translator and the text. This wrangling with translations, shown in the pencilled and penned-in additions and crossings out, displays an engaged mind, a working through, a carving out.

During my residency, translator and performance artist <u>Sophie Seita</u> and I devised a movement piece to perform in the foyer of the library – here are two lookalikes recreating it over Hamburger's words, over the crack. At their feet you'll see keyboards overlapping one another in a lightning-bolt shape, to be approached with achingly bent back to be rhythmically tapped; patterned ropes are entwined, untangled and reknotted like the different parts of a sentence;

transparent coloured sheets are held up and looked through and tried out, like finding the right tone to colour a book's reality.

Sophie and I were right in the middle of the floor, you couldn't miss us.

D5, D6, E7, E8 – Bandstand

Once, at the art fair where I was giving tours, I saw Kim Gordon of Sonic Youth giving a blazing guitar solo between the gallery stands; can you hear her, off in the distance? The Swiss punk band Kleenex also played in art galleries; I translated their guitarist's tour diaries along with reviews of and interviews with the band. My bands Monotony, which I played drums in, and Sauna Youth, which I sang and played a sampler in, would sometimes be invited to play shows in art galleries. We played at Modern Art Oxford and the Middlesbrough Institute of Modern Art. In fact, we're playing here tonight.

D.I.Y. music and art and literature are often intertwined; they come from the same place: making and doing and collaborating, the Gesamtkunstwerk of Do-It-Yourself culture. Playing in D.I.Y. punk bands was a way of making music, just like translating was a way of contributing to literature through my writing. But both of these creative pursuits have also been a vehicle for travelling the world and befriending hundreds of people, things I never thought I would do growing up.

All the people I've ever played with in bands started out as strangers – and even at the end of years of touring, there were bandmates who still felt mysterious to me. I got to know my over-a-dozen bandmates through the process of writing, rehearsing and performing. Each of us brought elements to the songwriting, and it would be a to-ing and fro-ing of compromise. I would come up with a drumbeat and it would be just right; other times people would make faces or mumble, and I would have to swallow my pride and change it up. I would bring lyrics I had worked hard to produce, and be prepared for half of them to change, for lines to be rewritten on the spot to fit properly with the music.

Some writers, readers and translators don't really think we translators can call ourselves 'co-authors' or that we have 'written' the book. How on earth could we call a translation 'collaboratively' written? We didn't, after all, create the characters or the plot or the sequence of events, or the original sentences. But we did write out the book again, from scratch. We had to pull it apart and rebuild it – the original book is useless to someone who cannot access it.

When you play in a band, unless you're an arsehole, you don't keep stressing which parts of the song you came up with – you write a song as a band. One person wrote the melody, one person wrote the lyrics, someone came up with the drumbeat, the bassline, another guitar line, the additional textures and sounds. You made the song together, the song exists because people worked together on it, and there should be no hierarchy of creation. Who is to say what the most integral part of the song is? How can we split the story from the words? If a reader reads a book in translation and says, 'I loved the way it was written', what then? It's both the author and translator who have made that happen. And I'm not speaking out of turn, or for my authors. One recently wrote in the acknowledgements to my translation of their book that the book was just as much mine. Authors frequently correct my 'your book' for 'our book', sometimes as if I have insulted them by not acknowledging the collaboration. Not all authors, not all.

In D.I.Y., you want to know how to do everything. Alongside making the music, there will be people in the scene or even in your band who can design the covers and the merch, screen-print the T-shirts and tote bags, write the copy, make the posters, organise gigs, do the sound, promote the show (this was done more and more on social media rather than flyers and posters). This led me to set up my own magazine and organise the launches, led me to promote my translations on social media, led me to start a press for Maltese literature in translation.

If you look up at the bandstand, you'll see how I was described in a music review, projected on the backdrop hanging at the back of the stage:

She cuts a nervous figure but her voice is an impressive instrument.

In bands from the age of nineteen, I whipped myself up into a state of confidence. I workshopped myself into not taking things personally and being flexible. Once you've found your voice, by which I mean your self, you want to embrace its strength in all places, both creatively and in everyday life.

I got an email from Grace Ambrose, a former editor of cult punk magazine *Maximum Rocknroll*, asking if I would be interested in translating *Das Tagebuch der Gitarristin Marlene Marder*, published in my translation under the title *The Diary of Marlene Marder*. It would make sense for me to be the book's translator, she reasoned, since the whole time I had been working as a literary translator from German to English I had also been playing and touring in D.I.Y. punk bands (it wasn't punk first, then translation – I would be reading books I was translating, and editing *New Books in German* magazine, even while touring in Europe and the USA). I knew German and I knew punk. I knew what a backline was and the various technical names for things on stage. I also knew what it was like to tour in a band, play in a band and be a woman in a band. I saw it as an opportunity to meld my two passions in a moment of feminist translation activism, and it felt right: punks translating punks being published by punks.

People often think that punk music is unskilled. I did too, until I met Richard and his enthusiasm for it was handed over to me. The metrics for skill are skewed. In punk and other kinds of hard rock music, it's not about technical, measurable skill but about drive, creativity, inclusivity. Grace's favourite line in my translation of Marlene Marder's diary was Marlene saying their playing is 'technically wrong, but with total conviction'.

When Meg White, the drummer of The White Stripes, who came out of the D.I.Y. rock scene, was mocked as being amateurish, Questlove of The Roots jumped to her defence: 'I try to leave "troll views" alone but this right here is out of line af [as fuck]. Actually what is wrong w[ith] music is people choking the life out of music like an Instagram filter – trying to reach a high of music perfection that doesn't even serve the song (or music).' It reminded me of an episode of *The Simpsons* when the Simpson family have to play in a band to pay off a restaurant bill: 'Your playing, while technically proficient, is lacking in passion.'

Writer Heather Perry speaks of the meeting place between learning to play music and learning a language:

> a revelation at my piano lesson today: the thing that's holding me back most is my terror of being bad at it, or getting caught out doing it 'wrong', which is ingrained from taking lessons as a kid & never quite feeling like I was doing it right. funny the things you realise. if you had lessons as a kid and you stared at the music thinking it was some language you'd never properly speak: there are other ways to learn!! and when you learn from listening and understanding chords and not obsessing about what's on the page – eventually you get it!

This idea that in order to be a musician, or a linguist, or a translator, you have to reach a level of extreme perfection is damaging and unhealthy and means you might not ever do it.

Soje speaks of thinking of their last translation draft as their 'penultimate' – the best draft, we must be aware, is unattainable.

A band takes the stage: The Translators. They're fronted by Layla Benitez-James, who stands at the mic and announces over feedback: 'There's just something that's really fun and almost punk about translation to me, that it's this impossible thing and yet we do it anyway.'

There's an infamous illustration from issue 1 of the punk fanzine *Sideburns*. It's by songwriter and guitar player Tony Moon and comprises scrawled sketches of three chords (A, E, G) and the words:

> This is a chord.
> This is another.

This is a third.
Now form a band.

'You didn't need to have been to music school or be particularly proficient or skilled. It was much more about the energy and drive to do something. It's a rallying call to the troops.' – Tony Moon

Here's mine:

HOW TO BECOME A TRANSLATOR
[three sketches of books scrawled on the wall]

This is a foreign language – start learning it.
[skip this step if you have more than one language]

This is a stack of books in both languages – start reading them.

Practise writing.

Now start translating.

Anyone can give it a try if they want to. Things change if you want others to see you *play*. If you want to take part outside your bedroom.

I think of Richard's pamphlet *D.I.Y. as Privilege: A Manifesto*, where we learn that it's all well and good to say D.I.Y. music is open to all, but there are barriers preventing or complicating people being able to 'do it themselves'. I think of *Folk Manifesta* by Lucy Wright, about how folk art has been co-opted by the middle and upper-middle classes to such a degree that no one wants folk art made by working-class folk artists, especially women, anymore. I think of *This Little Art* by Kate Briggs, where she queries whether a dance class – a metaphor she uses for translation – really is inclusive just because she is part of it.

There is luck, there is bias, there is fighting active exclusion, there can be finding your own people.

Automaton

Here's a life-sized wooden automaton of me. If you turn the handle, it begins to do repetitive compulsive movements. Its hand rises to the wood-shaving hair and twiddles it over and over. If you pull out a pin and shift down a lever in the back, it will start to type in the air. You can pull one of the hands till you hear a *click*, then the stick-like fingers will go limp, so that the fingers can flap against the palm when you pull the red string hanging from the elbow. These are my self-soothing stims to keep me from getting too mentally hyperactive; my parents invented the word 'twittering' for my twitching and hand flapping.

Clare Richards gave a great podcast interview about being neuro-divergent and a literary translator. She connects her autism diagnosis and literary translation, as they happened simultaneously. Her story sounds so similar to my story. We both had a younger brother diagnosed with autism at a very young age, but neither of us was ever considered to be on the autistic spectrum. Every job 'broke' her, she says; she could do them for a while, but not for a long period. She describes collapsing into depression and anxiety, and realising that perhaps she had struggled in those office environments because of being autistic.

As Clare says in the podcast, girls on the autistic spectrum learn to mask early on. I'm hyperaware that I have to 'act normally' all the time in public and social situations; it's like being in a foreign country and still trying to learn the local language and gestures and customs. I'm going to say this in chorus with Clare: 'I'd say, for me, translation is the only thing I could ever imagine myself doing at this point, translation almost wasn't a choice for me, this is the only career that I'm able to do given the ableist nature of the ordinary working place.'

Does my possibly being on the autistic spectrum and/or having ADHD make me a better or worse translator? Maybe it's why I can see patterns and layers, maybe it's why I can retain and recall a lot of particular kinds of information, why I enjoy how it uses all of my mental energy – and then some, like when I used to play drums and sing at the same time (sometimes I translate and sing at the same time). Maybe it means that because of burning out due to the nature of it, I don't feel secure and I chastise myself. I can notice tiny details in a text, but if my partner rearranges the furniture or puts a new picture up it might take me days to notice – I can't read the room.

Did I become a freelancer who works from home because of my job, or did I find the job so I could work from home? I found working in offices with strangers exhausting, almost painful. I can work surrounded by friends, by other translators or on my own, but not with anyone else.

Turn the wheel slower and slower until it comes to a stop.

Zoltar!

We borrowed and adapted Zoltar, the mechanical fortune teller from Playland. Our on-site engineers and puppeteers have remade this ethnically ambiguous, glass-encased, robotic fortune teller with our animatronic Michael Hofmann.

I first came across Hofmann when a friend at university gave me his translation of a collection of poems by the German poet Durs Grünbein. The written note inside said that as Hofmann was a very good poet in his own right, the translations must be good. This idea mesmerised me: that since he was a good writer, his writing skills would make the translations better; that translations are not automatically as good as the original book, no matter how exceptional the book is – they need a good writer behind them. I became so interested in where Hofmann was in his translation, I wrote my master's thesis about it.

My lecturer for Translation Theory, Theo Hermans – here represented by this wooden puppet in a shirt with rolled-up sleeves, white hair and glasses, dancing in front of Zoltar/Hofmann – announced at the beginning of his talk series that he wouldn't be supervising anyone's projects, and not to ask him. He also told everyone not to go into literary translation as it was so badly paid. I defied him twice.

Still painfully unable to speak up in or after class, I went to see him in his office and asked if he would *please* supervise my thesis, he had so much energy and enthusiasm for translation and I loved all his lectures. He begrudgingly agreed. One of his favourite analogies for the translator's voice was thinking about Rachel-from-*Friends*/Jennifer Aniston. We can see Rachel in other characters that Aniston plays because, when it comes down to it, Rachel is Aniston, and we can see Aniston in all her characters. If we're honest, we go to see films not just for the characters but to see our favourite actors playing them, because we recognise that they bring something to the character.

After my master's, I read Hofmann's other translations to read him. I also read the anthology of essays written about him, and his essays.

I read his letters to editors, where he talked back against their inexpert criticism of his work. He had thought about everything so thoroughly, he knew exactly what he was doing, and I wanted to do the same.

Instead of providing your fortune, the Hofmann machine will give you a slip of paper with a quote from my favourite essay on translation, his 'Sharp Biscuit'. His line about the words he uses in his translations being words he's 'knocked around with', like they're personal friends. The line where he says that the act of service for a translator is 'writing as well and as interestingly as possible'. And my personal favourite, regarding the unstoppable, undeniable, subtle influence of the translator on a translated text, he summarises himself (myself) as: '"has written the occasional modern poem" but also "likes punk"'.

Every dozen plays on the Hofmann machine, he will recite his speech from when he won the big translation award for his translation of Jenny Erpenbeck, where he said that being a translator is like being the back end of a pantomime horse.

Every once in a while, he'll say about Kafka, 'In any case, he remains, I hope, an author to read, not someone for experts.'

Whenever I feel like I'm not sure about this whole thing, I put a coin in the slot.

Z27 – Clown School

Bring in the clowns!

Come on everyone, choose an outfit, our face painters will get you ready, grab a nose! *Honk!*

Come through the curtain with the embroidered quote from the film *Young Frankenstein*:

> Frederick Frankenstein: It's terrible the price that society demands
> in the name of fidelity, isn't it? I mean, what is fidelity, after all?
> Inga: Not fooling around?

A lot of people in literature take themselves very seriously. I always thought that you had to be a serious person to be a writer and translator. I would go to events and see these serious people with their impenetrable mask of knowledge – including Michael Hofmann – and think, I'll never be able to do this.

But then I realised I could do this, and I was still a ridiculous person. I could still watch *Labyrinth* and eat ice cream and dress up at Halloween and do silly voices and impressions and play in bands. When I teach translation or talk about translation at events, one of my aims is to be approachable, which is different from when I'm performing on stage in bands, where I wanted to appear aggressively happy.

I'm living proof that you can spend your evenings and weekends screaming your head off on a stage and be friendly-silly and approachable on a panel, while also being a closed-off and introverted person in everyday life. The way I clown is political to me. Being unshowy but present on a stage, and then being approachable to an audience that might include someone intimidated by the performance of aloof intellectualism, is important. Whenever I perform anything – a song, at a panel discussion, how I present myself – I'm always undercutting something.

I'm glad because I can now say this clown, this unserious person, this person without a prestigious education and no connections and no additional support, has done well.

On either side of this clown car, you can read the Q&A from an interview with Soje about their zine *chogwa*, which published multiple translations of the same poem.

> JY: You write, 'I knew that the existence of other translations would [...] dare us to be a little cheekier.' I think of playful exuberance and taking pleasure in translation as two of my favorite characteristics of *chogwa*. Why are qualities like playfulness and cheekiness important to you as a translator?
> Soje: The term 장난꾸러기, or 장꾸 [janggu] comes to mind – someone who likes mischief and play! I consider myself a janggu. I love teasing; I like levity and mischief. I think that extends to my work as well. I don't like heaviness or pretentiousness, especially for myself. I like being a fool and the idea that nothing is set in stone.

One of our clowns lifts up his long shoe and shows a quote from someone online printed onto the sole:

> I would like to read an eloquent, no-bullshit translation of the *Iliad*.

Wait until they find out that all translations are absolutely full of bullshit. *Translation as bullshitting.*

I sometimes imagine that at the start or end of every line in my translations, it says: 'I'm pretty sure they're saying', or '...I reckon'. It's the same reflex as when we're talking to someone about any bit of writing and we qualify it with a, 'What I think the author is saying...'. It doesn't mean that we're completely unsure – we're sure enough to say it, aren't we; we didn't say 'I have no idea what they mean' – but that there's at least a shadow of a caveat. I'm not the author, and even the author isn't always sure what they meant, or sure of all the influences on what they've expressed. What a bunch of clowns we are! Having a right laugh.

A critic with a couple of translations under their belt complained that Emily Wilson's translation of the *Odyssey* was too plot-driven and that they wanted it to be more like the text was at the time it was written. This is a clownish remark. A translation can only be made in the cognition of the time it is entering and the place it is entering. They're asking to have a text not of its time and not of its place, which is basically the original. Why don't you learn Ancient Greek and go back to Ancient Greece? *Honk!*

T2052 – Laser Quest

Put on your visors and pick up your guns. One of you has a red laser, the other a green laser. You have to find as many mistakes as you can in the text on the screen. 3... 2... 1... *GO!*

After being an au pair for about three months in Munich, one of the worst experiences of my life, I got a temp job at the European Patent Office. I was nineteen and in my own enormous, glass-walled office, which had been empty for years due to understaffing and looked out on to the Deutsches Museum. It looked incredible during winter when it snowed. I would daydream that it was a fairy-tale castle and I was on top of a mountain, deciding whether to descend.

My job was to receive edited and proofread documents with mark-ups on them, find the document in the system, make the changes electronically, print out the document and show it to my boss. I could see how the editors had made their changes to these letters and speeches about patents, so though I was only inputting the data, I was also being given an editing and proofreading masterclass. It was meant to last only a couple of months, but I ended up staying for six. Everyone had a soft spot for me because I was young, and they found it humorous that I would come to work after staying out all night at gigs. My friends were patent lawyers in their thirties, who were funny and silly and yet still lawyers. They introduced me to espresso and gossip and took care of me. By the end, I was editing and proofreading documents myself.

Did any of you pick up the Fair Guide on your way in? You didn't see one? Maybe we didn't do one? Just after my undergraduate degree, I applied for an unpaid editorial internship based at a large art gallery. For my interview, I had to sit a proofreading exam, where they gave me a blown-up double-page spread from the gallery's exhibition guide and I had to mark up everything I could find. I scored 120 per cent, having found things they hadn't considered. I got the placement.

It was supposed to be one day a week for three months. I was back living with my parents in Shoreham-by-Sea, so would get the cheap train up the night before and stay with old uni friends so I could be there on time. They offered to extend my placement because they appreciated my work, they said I could stay as long as I wanted, but I limited it to two more months as that was what I could afford.

During my time there, I progressed from proofreading to writing copy for the guide on the main exhibitions. I learnt about colour proofing, printing and style guides. I got to assist the photographer, taking day-long strolls around the gallery chatting, the back of me appearing in many photos because, he said, 'people like to picture themselves viewing art'. It was always uncanny to see these photos printed in the guide, me in relation to fine art.

A friend of a friend, Joe Hales (who designed the poster for the Fair), was assisting the head designer on the other side of the room, and this was where we really got to know one another. I told him about wanting to make a magazine about Anglo-German culture called *Verfreundungseffekt*. He offered to design it all for free so he could try out his designs. The gallery photographer gave me a piece for it, as did someone I worked with at the clothes shop in Brighton. There was a piece I translated by my German ex, illustrations by my future housemates and my boss at the gallery, all these people who had been part of my life so far.

I started to feel like I was homing in on something. *Pew, pew, pew!*

There is an affirmative mantra running through a speaker on the outside of this empty booth with a microphone on a stand:

> Tell yourself, 'My translation is giving published, it's serving literary masterpiece', hype yourself up today! – <u>Adrienne Bruce</u>

Can anyone do impressions, impersonations? I'll give one a go…

After publishing an essay about translating Gregor Hens's memoir *Nicotine*, I found a below-the-line comment:

> I started reading *Nicotine* a couple of days ago and I must say I like it a lot. One thing which came to mind while reading the first chapter is that the narrator/author sounds a lot older than he actually is. I was sure he's over the age of 60 until I looked up Gregor Hens in Google. Also, while the questions you raise about translating a book about smoking whilst being a non-smoker yourself are valid I also wonder how easy it is to translate a man's voice being a woman.

I, too, was surprised when I saw that Gregor Hens was a man in his forties when he wrote his memoir; the voice of the book feels a lot older, I agree. His style feels more mature than his real, human years, and more sombre, in a way, than his true persona. But that's the thing: a text is not the person who writes it, it's a construct, and over time we attribute a gendered and aged nature to it.

I think a lot of women, including myself, feel well versed in older men's writing because it's what we grew up with – 'we speak the language of men', Meryl Streep says on a panel, to bemused looks from male actors – my formative years and beyond were saturated by reading books by men. I can 'put on' a 'male writer's voice' in a text.

I feel there are many kinds of knowledge and multiple perspectives, many layers to novels, many valid interpretations and approaches and priorities, and therefore many valid translators and translations. There is working-class knowledge, there is the intimate knowledge of having close relatives living with mental illness, there is the knowledge of being a creative writer and writer of poetry, there is the knowledge formed through living as a woman. All these knowledges were very necessary in the translating of *Tanz am Kanal*, *Dance by the Canal*, by Kerstin Hensel, the third book and first novel I translated.

One of the most useful and difficult aspects of these knowledges was having experienced sexual harassment and assault. *Dance by the Canal* includes multiple sexual assaults, including rape, possibly two, in fact, depending on interpretation, as well as an adult violin teacher forcibly kissing the main character, Gabriela, as a child (whether this 'really' happens is beside the point in the context of reading the account of it). There is a particular incident in the novella that felt harder and harder to work on every time I reached it during the drafting process.

In the novella, Gabriela is raped by two men in a park. The first time I translated the scene, I got déjà vu. It reminded me of when I was walking through a park in Munich one night when I was eighteen and a man tried to rape me. I translated this experience into a poem called 'Taking a Walk'. Near the beginning of the poem is the line, 'I walk through parks at four in the morning / to wear the noiseless monochrome and warm greys of the city', and later the 'I' of the poem recalls my memory: 'A man brought me down by the ankle once / by a giant metal chess set.' The man had grabbed my leg from behind and pulled it up, while simultaneously pushing me off the path onto the grass. I was shocked and winded for a moment but rolled over quickly before he could sit on my back. I pulled my leg back and kicked at him, but missed, and felt something wrench in my calf muscle. I had learnt at karate lessons when I was younger how to twist my hands at the wrist to get out of grips, and while he tried to pin me down, I kicked him in the side of the head with my other leg. I got up and hobble-ran out the park like someone hungry for life, down a yard and into a stinking shed where communal bins were kept for a block of flats. I stayed there until the sun came up and a resident came to drop their rubbish off on their way to work. I made them jump, looming out of the dark.

I don't elaborate on what happened to me after that line about the ankle and the chess set, because I know the reader will already know what it means for a woman to be knocked down in a park by a man. That we know, as a society, what it means, what is inferred, how to fill in the blanks, should mean something, at least to those who understand these silences. Reading and rereading the rape scene in the novella I was translating became more and more difficult with every draft. I wanted it to be true to the horrific assault, it was part of my job not only to translate the words but to translate the experience: might someone unaware of the brutality of rape translate 'Schmerz' as 'twinge' or 'ache' rather than 'pain'? But for my mind to translate this scene accurately, my body would call upon my instincts, my muscle memory. Do you mean this? As I reread the scene, I would relive what happened to me in the park and all the alternative worse scenarios and all the times I've been touched inappropriately by men, including friends. I would even relive the stiffening of my body from the time a male friend said he had never seen a woman being harassed in the street, not once – myself and the other women present groaned that we experienced and noticed it all the time. My body started to tense up and cramp, my skin would buzz, it felt like someone was scratching the underside of my stomach. If you're reliving that, my body expressed, maybe you'd like to relive this? The scene became inseparable from my own experience, the terrible ending that was supposed to happen. This buried memory started to fester, become more and more toxic. Words were now enough to set off a physical reaction in me, be they in fiction or in the news. I can't help but analyse texts, and that analysis happens in my body, too.

This book left behind its own kind of muscle memory, one that conversely limited a fight or flight reflex; a honed muscle for translating books where the priority is to explore cultural and personal trauma through disorientating narrative experiences. It helped me hold back the instinct to panic if what I was reading wasn't giving me a discernible narrative or a clear purpose or spelled-out information. Working on *Dance by the Canal* trained me to trust all the component parts, even if I couldn't see the links until perhaps the second or third read, the second or third draft. This, my first novel translation, took twelve drafts, twelve relivings.

The Ungeziefer in the Room

Here's a big papier-mâché metamorphosed Gregor Samsa, six feet high and twelve feet long, lying on its back with its legs in the air. It's obviously *indescribable*, and each of you will see it slightly differently. <u>Damion Searls</u> talks of reading and translating as being analogous to phenomenology: we each see or read a finite thing, that's for sure, but we all have different experiences of it, with infinite nuances and differentials.

In the last year of my undergrad degree, I took a module in modernist literature and we looked at Kafka's *The Metamorphosis*, which I hadn't read since those few pages during my A-levels in the broom cupboard. I was too shy to speak in seminars, would feel like I was going to explode with repressed comments, but couldn't release them. After one class, I hung back to blurt out to the tutor how fascinating it was reading the introduction and notes to the edition we were reading, about how to translate 'ungeheures Ungeziefer', the description of transformed Gregor Samsa. This translation conundrum compelled me to finally speak, to say something, because this fascination was completely genuine – there are multiple translations for the same thing in different editions, which must mean there are various translations for everything in translation! There were other books we read in translation, and, as with Kafka, we never engaged with them as translations; this was apparently irrelevant, beside the point.

Hanging up on the wall next to the sculpture are a number of headphones. You can listen to a twelve-minute radio programme where the British playwright Jeff Young talks about his fascination with *The Metamorphosis*; reading it was a 'transformative' experience for him in his youth.

It's so good to listen to him enthuse about Kafka. Early on in the programme he misquotes a translation of Kafka's famous line, saying that we must take an axe to 'the frozen sea beneath us', but it's actually 'within us' or 'inside us'. But that's a blip. A fan of Marvel comics and superheroes, he understands Gregor Samsa being transformed not by radiation but by 'a loathing for his job'.

We learn that as a child, Young didn't think about books being written – I too couldn't imagine how books were written as a child – and that words surely 'fell between the pages of books'. We also share the lack of knowing as children that books were written in foreign languages and that someone translated them.

Then the bug hits the zapper.

Young proceeds to go into detail about seeing the words of a German-language edition of Kafka's stories after having read an English translation:

> *I think*, even though I couldn't read German, that seeing the words on the page in this strange language gave me a closer understanding of Kafka's intentions. He thought in a different language and saw the world in a different language to me. I thought I could never really understand Kafka's stories because I couldn't get close enough to his thoughts. I didn't trust the translator. My Kafka stories were translated by Edwin and Willa Muir. How did I know they were telling the true story? I had the feeling that there was a space in between the German-language telling of the tale and its English translation, somewhere intangible, a mysterious zone of misunderstanding. Kafka couldn't have known about this zone because he didn't know his stories would be translated. But for me, it's this zone between two languages that increases the uncertainty and tension. The only way to be certain of Kafka's intentions is to read his stories in the language they were written. But I was thrilled by the uncertainty.

What Young says speaks to the shared, wider paranoia about translated books, and a phenomenon I've noticed whereby readers feel so protective of an author that they think that a translator can't possibly know the writer's work as well as they do or the author does. There's also the concept here that there is one core reading of a foreign-language book that needs to be found and reiterated by the translator. When I say 'Young' from this point on, I'm quoting him but I'm not blaming him. I'm using 'Young' as an umbrella for those who share his 'Youngian thinking' on translation, those who are monolingual and/or not translators.

Young talks in binaries. A word used in translation is either 'well chosen' or 'mischosen', but the truth is that there are usually many 'well-chosen' words, selected for a specific purpose; of course there might be the odd, rare mischosen word – that is inevitable.

Young paints the many translators of *The Metamorphosis* as 'hesitant and uncertain' (they can't have been that hesitant or uncertain, their choices are in print in a published book), even though most of them have argued clearly as to why they chose their words for Ungeziefer, like 'vermin', 'bug', 'insect' – umbrella terms for unwanted visitors that an exterminator would destroy – and 'cockroach', a more specific term but used to dehumanize people.

'gigantic insect' (Muir & Muir, 1933); 'monstrous insect' (Bernofsky, 2014); 'monstrous vermin' (Corngold, 1972; Neugroschel, 1993; Crick, 2009); 'monstrous cockroach' (Hofmann, 2007); 'enormous bedbug' (Moncrieff, 2014); 'large verminous insect' (Williams, 2014).

They are all correct – and note that Columbia University professor and translator Susan Bernofsky chooses the same word, 'insect', that those rascally Muirs had alighted on seventy-odd years earlier.

I think Young actually calls the translators hesitant and uncertain because of the nature of translation and of translators – he doesn't like the fact that translation changes its mind. Translation is never fixed, and translators must not jump in and must never be totally certain. One of my mottos while translating is *think again*.

The words Young uses to 'translate' the transformed Gregor Samsa – 'the creature', 'a creature with an untranslatable name' – are mischosen, a mistranslation, a misrepresentation, and this is because he can't read German. Ungeziefer cannot be translated as creature, and has been translated an array of correct ways.

Young then goes after the Muirs, who translated *The Metamorphosis* nearly a hundred years ago:

> I read somewhere that the Muirs weren't particularly fluent in German and that they took on the translation job because they needed the cash. Is Kafka drab and perfunctory because Edwin and Willa Muir's life was? I imagine them huddled at a kitchen table in their dressing gowns ripping the books in half, scribbling and crossing out words with pencil stubs in a dimly lit apartment somewhere in Germany, ignoring the bills piling up on the doormat, making the world Kafkaesque for English readers.

Ironically, he makes Willa and Edwin Muir into dusty, slimy Ungeziefer. Young misuses – on purpose, by accident – available information about the Muir translation duo's language skills. It came out in Willa's diaries and her book *Belonging* that Edwin didn't really know German very well and that she did the majority of the translation work, and that Edwin had a tendency not to correct people when they received dual credit. They really did rip books in half to share translation duties. This might be a shock, but all working translators take on translations because of the cash, because it's our job; that we choose to be translators because we're passionate and good at it is also true. Who promoted the idea that an artist shouldn't get paid for their work? I translated Wim Wenders for money in my pyjamas at the kitchen table during my drab little life; sometimes I would delete things and rewrite bits – that's what writing and translating is. I'm always turning lights off and putting off putting on the heating to keep the bills low. The Muirs really did help the Anglosphere become Kafkaesque, and not only in translations – they were the ones who read, championed and pitched Kafka's *Das Schloss*/*The Castle* to a publisher, who took on the rights and got them to translate it.

Young talks about how much *The Metamorphosis* changed his life and how it reinvigorates his work. So strange. So strange because he would not be able to be inspired by Kafka without translators, no matter what he thinks; he would not be able to get inspired by *The Metamorphosis* via osmosis.

At the end of the programme, Young reads his 'literal translation' of the opening sentence of *The Metamorphosis*; it's a non-translation, just raw mismatched elements strung together. He admits he still doesn't know what Kafka intended, and yet his conclusion is that he still doesn't trust Kafka's translators:

> There is something slightly 'Kafkaesque' about the role of the translator as she negotiates a transaction from one language to another. [...] There is a degree of sleight of hand conjuring about the art of converting a word into a different kind of word. We have to take it on trust that translators are responsible practitioners of magic.

It's all a bit 'burn the witch'. What was that that just flew over our heads? So many readers have trust issues with translators. What if we started from the point of trust, from the benefit of the doubt? From the assumption that we translators know what we're doing, that we've proceeded with care?

I will most likely never be asked to translate Kafka, but if I were, and in the knowledge that there are so many English translations available, I'd be tempted to do a version where Samsa wakes up to find he was a 'goblin'. I wrote a book about goblins, how vague and ambiguous they look and are, and can imagine it working quite nicely in the 'goblin mode' zeitgeist. It would also link up with an interpretation of the book as being about antisemitism, as the figure of the goblin, like the figure of the cockroach or vermin, has an extensive history of being an antisemitic trope.

When Gregor Samsa awoke one morning from disturbing dreams, he found himself in his bed shapeshifted into some kind of goblin. (My translation)

'Some kind of' is kind of like 'monstrous' because we don't know what it is, and that's scary... But in fact, if we think about it, 'goblin' wouldn't be a translation of 'Ungeziefer', it would be a translation of the word 'creature' that gets used by Young and others and which has come out of the idea, the myth, that 'Ungeziefer' can't be translated, when it can be and has. I could use 'goblin' because of the *perception* of The Metamorphosis, but I can read German, I can read and research this word, and it would be unacceptable in a standard literary translation. It would be fun, though, it would speak to something in the process of happening, it would be an easy and gratifying connection to the reader right now. A translation is of its time, and of its translator – in any case, there is no neutral choice.

The poet Lemn Sissay collaborated with the director Scott Graham on a theatre adaptation of *The Metamorphosis*, calling it in an interview a work about 'modern living'. They read the novella as being about masculinity, family, work and class, a story about a man who is worn down by being a breadwinner and living in debt, but also about Gregor's sister Grete, who is laughed at by the lodger for thinking that she could be a violinist with her working-class background.

'What is shown to be ridiculous is someone like Grete holding a violin. That's when the family realise the system is crushing them,' Graham says. He continues:

I'm from a working-class background and that's why it struck a chord with me. Look at our education system and the way that the arts are being devalued in such an insidious way. What they're doing is teaching the working classes to devalue the arts themselves. It's a different thing from your Eddie Redmaynes [educated at Eton] or those from that background who are encouraged to make art.

Sissay is asked whether this promotes the trope of the artist working for the love of it, rather than the money: 'I find it funny that people think we should work for free, just for the love of it. I get people who assume – because they assume the arts is a luxury – that you have another life and the art is what you do on the side.'

A burned-out citizen is an Ungeziefer, a working-class artist is an Ungeziefer. In one of the books I'm translating now, a burned-out-man's flat is infested with Ungeziefer; small white worms, ants, moths. Creepy crawlies?

Within the last few weeks, the word used by Kafka to describe Gregor Samsa in his new form has been used in the German media to describe Palestinians during the reporting of a 'ceasefire' from Israeli bombardment. A woman shouting at 'Menschen mit Migrationshintergrund' – 'people with a migration background' – on a Berlin U-Bahn train called them 'Ungeziefer' and said that they should all be killed.

Pick a translation for the word 'Ungeziefer' in these above new contexts, where those being described are human beings:

VERMIN
RATS
SCUM

Ungeziefer is something specific, and it is always changing, always gaining new meanings, new histories. But it's never good.

I think of Gregor Samsa lying in his bed and I can't help but think of The Metamorphosis as a book about illness, I can't help but think about my mum, or more specifically, how certain people would think of my mum, how certain people might translate the subtext of 'Ungeziefer' as parasite, freeloader, drain on society. As a translator, you have to think how others might think, inhabit the character, no matter how monstrous.

A8 – Grab Her!

Let's approach this contraption.

Oiling the cogs is my dad. He looks after all the machinery here at the Fair. The contraption looks like a giant version of those grabber machines you get in arcades, the ones that are always rigged.

We've got something! My mum!

When she is being moved in and out of bed she looks like a cuddly toy, a prize. Every time she's hoisted into the air, she's surprised, because between each hoist she forgets it exists because of her rapidly developing dementia, a symptom, we'll learn later in an autopsy – a certain translation of my mother – of an undetected blood infection. She is either concerned, like she's at the top of a rollercoaster that's going to plummet at any moment, or finds it wonderful, like she's floating off in a hot air balloon.

My mum now shreds her patterns, her knitting is a large, tangled heap of different coloured wool that she picks at with the same concentration and care as she did with her knitting. She grabs a handful and says that it's for my partner to wear. My dad has to watch her because she's started putting wool and scraps of knitting patterns in her mouth, trying to eat it.

I too have mistaken my work as nourishment.

When someone is losing their grip on reality, we say their mind is unravelling. When a narrative seems to lose its way, we might say that this was the point when the story unravelled. Will I one day sit and tear up books and call it reading? Shred a novel and say I'm translating it? And look full of focus, determination, satisfaction, the same as if I were actually doing it? This thought actually brings me comfort, as shredding and pulling does for my mum. Free from the responsibility of creating a product for sale, she can just enact the soothing motions of creation.

My mum consults the knitting pattern, jotting down a note, knitting a line, unravelling it, over and over. The note is always the same, the line is always undone. The writer Sophie Mackintosh says, 'knitting … it's woolly Valium', and that unravelling four hours of work is OK because it's more about the process. Someone who could fluently knit a complex pattern full of woollen twists, braids, bobbles, who could recreate pom-poms in wool, whole scarves and thick jumpers in days or weeks, is lost for stitches, can no longer complete anything. How can I turn my own mum into a metaphor? Well, my mum has always been a story told by others, a myth from my childhood, and 'mum' doesn't accurately describe her relation to me. For a long time I called her Margaret and she flinch-laughed, her own name like a needle. I used to annoy my brother by being able to figure out the endings to *Jonathan Creek* episodes when we watched them as a family. I have always known how my mum's story would end. I see more and more how I am a translation of my parents, how I am the story of both their lives, including the legacies of their own unexplored preoccupations and traumas.

My mum now only speaks in half-words, sounds. She will say what sounds like a question, or like she's making a point, but it is just random shards of syllables, and she will look to me expectantly for an answer, and as long as I say something resembling one, she's satisfied and will say something else. When translating, often it is mostly that the line sounds right, or I focus on the pattern of sound and what it's doing in the original, and then focus on the sound in the translation, not the exact words. If it's a question, it must sound like a question, if it's an uncertain answer, it must sound like an uncertain answer, if it's a joke, people have got to laugh. You've got to laugh, no matter what.

My mum was diagnosed with schizophrenia and manic depression when she was in her late teens. My dad's mum was also a schizophrenic, a result of PTSD from growing up as a teenager during the blitz in Malta. There is a history of mental illness and addiction in my family, and I've been navigating that, as in, wondering when it's my turn. Sometimes if I get too stressed while translating a book – it can be unimaginably stressful – I add to the stress by worrying: will this be what tips my sanity over the edge?

My mum was in and out of psychiatric facilities during my childhood. I remember asking her, when I was small, what it was like hearing voices. It was quite nice, she said, they weren't scary, they kept her company. My days are filled with fictional voices, stories, authors beside me in my head, daydreaming is a huge part of my job. I like to think my mum's day-to-day life is on some level similar to mine, that we have something in common. Have I channelled her inherited mind into a job? What would I do without writing and translating? What would become of me? My mum used to like painting and drawing, what would have happened if she had become an artist? I know it's not as simple as that; just because writing and translating sustains my mind, it doesn't mean art could have saved her. But I think her problems started when she was misread when she was young, and that started a certain kind of story.

Tenses might shift or slip in translation. This should have been written in the past.

Bins/Trashcans

The bins around the Fair are in the shape of big pretzels with smiling faces. Rubbish goes in their mouths. Each pretzel is holding up a flag bearing a statement about mistakes.

There was never an error-free text.

From *Possession* by A.S. Byatt, where students transcribe passages by a writer.

They're not mistakes they're imperfections in the fabric of existence reminding us that to be alive is to be flawed.
– <u>Jeremy Tiang</u>

In Wenders: *incorrect Italian!*

Wenders had got the one word of Italian wrong in the original and I copied it over because I presumed it was correct and I don't speak Italian. An editor could have double checked it, but they didn't!

In Hens: *adding in an illustration where there wasn't one in the original!*

The illustration being referenced is famous in Germany, but not here in the UK. Without it, the meaning would be incomplete, it would be an incomplete translation.

In Edelbauer: *the table metaphor seems weird to me!*

I have a bit of French. I bought the French translation of Edelbauer's German novel purely to see how the French translator had dealt with a particular metaphor about a stack of papers on a desk being like a pool. When I turned to the corresponding page, I found that the French translator had dealt with the metaphor by simply removing it from the book. It makes me think of <u>Ursula Le Guin</u> on translation: 'The metaphors all self-destruct'!

In Hensel: *in the translation, a character fails to die!*

...because this character reappears alive later in the book, a confirmed error by the author!

In Marder: *you said a character was dead when they weren't!*

Only in the first draft, and only because Tod (death) and Ted (Teddy Boy) look similar at a glance!

In Meyerhoff: *you mistranslated a word!*

Again, only in a draft, and the German-speaking editor picked it up! I had read a simile about an IV drip as 'intravenous seaweed' – seaweed is 'Algen' – because I'd misread where the words in the compound impacted. German can make a new word from two or three or many more put together. I thought it was a strange image. Maybe it's referring to the translucency of the bag of fluid, I thought, or the lines hanging down like trailing seagrass? Maybe I should adapt it to jellyfish? The editor *liked the mistake.*

'This is funny,' the editor wrote to me, 'because it works with "Algen" as well! However, in the original it's "Galgen" – would "intravenous gallows" work? Or do you have a better suggestion?'

Would it have been so bad if it had been intravenous seaweed?

In Poschmann – *the wrong type of tail/tale! In a published, award-nominated translation!*

Yes, this one did make it into the final translation. One of my mentees told me that her absolute favourite line in a book I translated was where a 'tale goes around a corner' as a fox leaves the scene, but it should have been his literal 'tail'.

What does it mean if that's her favourite line in a book and it's a mistake?

Have you learnt how to use pass and passed yet?!

No.

I remember being at dinner with an ex-boyfriend and his snooty, posh uncle. The uncle asked me what I was studying:

Media and English, I said.
Remedial English, he repeated, nodding sadly at his mishearing.
Don't worry, you'll get there in the end.

Let's rifle through the precious trash, full of discarded drafts and research print-outs. Unscrunch this essay, 'Trash Talk: On Translating Garbage' by Lina Mounzer, about how the worst thing to translate is a bad text. You can't translate something that is empty, that's purely bunches of letters cloaking the fact that the writer is saying nothing. Translators can spot a fake text from a mile off, just words without the meaning stitching them together. Translator Jocelyne Allen says:

> We don't talk about this enough in translation, but sometimes, the source text is nonsense and we are forced to make sense of it as translators. We have to piece something halfway meaningful together bc [because] no one ever blames the source text for its incoherence; it's always the translation that's wrong.

It's like: have you ever read a book? An article, a poem? Sometimes they're not good, not great, not spectacular. Working with a bad text as a foundation means it will always remain a bad text; you can't polish a turgid text.

JB1 – Catch the Red Herring!

If you can catch the red herring in the tank full of fish with your rod you win a prize!

I often say that words, when translating a text, are a red herring. The name of the red herring is <u>John Berger</u>. John Berger put forward the idea that translators don't translate words, we translate that mysterious place where the words originated:

> True translation is not a binary affair between two languages but a triangular affair. The third point of the triangle being what lay behind the words of the original text before it was written. True translation demands a return to the pre-verbal. One reads and rereads the words of the original text in order to penetrate through them to reach, to touch, the vision or experience that prompted them. One then gathers up what one has found there and takes this quivering almost wordless 'thing' and places it behind the language it needs to be translated into.

Or, we could paraphrase this into the words of Jeremy Tiang:

> I don't care about the 'meanings' of 'words' I'm out here translating ~~~vibes~~~

Today at the Kino we're showing the short film adaptation of my short story 'The Natural'.

When the actor Charlie Rowe bought the rights to adapt my story 'The Natural' into a short film, it was like when my friend and former bandmate <u>Maria Tedemalm</u> translated some of my poems into Swedish; I heard within these acts: *you didn't just entertain me or interest me, you inspired me*, and this made me reconsider how I feel about the authors I choose to translate – they inspire me, with their great writing, to create something.

When I watch and rewatch Charlie's short film, about an aspiring actor who can't help but make people laugh, it is my story, but made of a different fabric. Certain things have changed – the heritage of the famous Marianne has changed from Maltese to English, the location is not Glasgow but London. Are these details irrelevant? They were carefully chosen in my story, and yet I don't think anything has been lost in the adaptation. I can see that Charlie – who also stars as the main character Willem (without bowtie, without mascara) – has completely understood the story inside and out. We talked over Zoom when he had finished his screenplay, and when he talked about the story, about how much he could relate to Willem, I knew I could trust him.

Of course, my story still exists, and is available to read, alongside Charlie's film. But arguably, when something is translated into film, it's like when something is translated into English: it becomes more accessible to more people, it in some way eclipses the original.

Next up is the film adaptation of *The Reader*, starring Kate Winslet and Ralph Fiennes. Later: *Die Hard* and *Die Hard with a Vengeance*, starring Alan Rickman and Jeremy Irons.

Translation School

I'd like to open a Translation School, or the School of Adaptation. It would be like art school, or writing school, where any creative practitioner would not only understand from a place of creativity, but understand how creativity is a transformed energy, that it always comes from something else, from abstract ideas, from images and experiences, other people, and what that means in a creative sense, an ethical sense. Everyone would learn a language, everyone would read mostly texts about translation, everyone would make something in one form and then try and make it into another, a poem into a film, a text in one language into another language. A translation-led curriculum, taught by literary translators and adapters and audio-describers and screenwriters, translation, translation, translation. Everyone would go out into the world saying, 'it's like translation', with this dreamy look on their face, instead of or alongside, 'it's like music', 'it's like poetry'.

This is just a cardboard playhouse, like the one my brother and I made when we were kids and lived in for a whole weekend.

Push the walls, they'll give way.

And behind it you'll find...

Gift Shop Stand

Aprons so you can tell when you're translating and when you're not translating.

Books provided by The Hastings Bookshop (a great supporter of translated literature and small presses, recently closed down, but still open here).

Stick-on tattoos based on my translation-related tattoos (many translators have translation-related tattoos: Emily Wilson, Deborah Smith...):

the skull of St Jerome (the patron saint of translators)
an ü, for German, done by Richard
Jacques Derrida's equation of translation, $S=P$ (the instance where languages are both different and the same), within a beflowered envelope
a ladle illustration by Fi Jae Lee from the cover of the poetry collection *Autobiography of Death* by Kim Hyesoon, translated by Don Mee Choi
the cover illustration of a woman drinking a beer from my translation of Michelle Steinbeck's novel
a TV, a translation of a short story by Anna Weidenholzer into a tattoo designed by Martha Ellen Smith.

All but three of these tattoos are by Martha Ellen Smith, who said, the last time I saw her, that she was proudly explaining to someone what literary translation is, based on our numerous conversations during tattooing...

Charm bracelets of all the words used to describe my translations in reviews, an object imagined by Ann Goldstein in an interview.

My charms include:

ably
expertly
impeccably
pitch-perfect
rollicking
shaky

Most reviews don't mention how I'm doing at all.

Here is a stack of screen-printed posters you can take away. The poster reads: *Nothing is translatable, we're just trying our best* – Jeremy Tiang, which Khairani Barokka had shared online, allowing me to see it.

As I write on my tax return every year: I've tried my best. I suppose that could be interpreted two ways: I tried my best to complete my tax return, and I tried my best to earn a living, even if it doesn't seem that way.

Behind the Gift Shop Stand – Portrait of Myself

Richard recently came across a painting of Willa Muir in a gallery; it's maybe the only painting of a translator I've heard of apart from one of Michael Hofmann – and St Jerome with his pet skull, they're everywhere.

Here on the back wall of the gift shop stand is a portrait of me painted by Richard earlier on in our relationship. There couldn't be an exhibition of myself without a painting of me...

I have prepared an audio-description of the painting, as I have for all the rooms and sculptures in the Fair, for blind and visually impaired visitors:

> This painting in oils is rectangular and in a dark wooden tray frame. The longer sides are around 40 cms. The brushstrokes are fine and choppy, it looks like it's been knitted, or collaged out of tiny slats of painted wood. A face emerges from this carefully layered mark-making. A head and shoulders are visible. The face has a blank expression and is looking slightly to the right. The figure has shoulder-length dark wavy hair, dark arched eyebrows, a small mouth and chin, a large angular nose, jutting cheekbones, large dark eyes, and they are wearing a dark blue jumper. There is a light blue background that hints at brickwork, with a mysterious red line running across the bottom centimetre of the painting.

I can feel the time and attention that Richard put into translating me into paint – his understanding of me – emanating warmly from this painting. I felt like I had become a real person when I saw this painting. A painting says: you're worth recording.

This concludes our tour. I've enjoyed being your guide, taking you around the book/fair. It's what I do every day, really, guiding people around a book they can't yet fathom, step by step.

I wanted to build this Fair because I wasn't sure where to put all *this stuff*, and storage is expensive. I would like to thank the fabricators and the installation team, the stunt coordinator, the cleaning staff, the catering staff, the architects, the illustrators, the lighting designers, the actors, the PR person, the shop assistant, all those behind the scenes… I would like to thank you for being my test audience.

I might have to follow one of you guys out, though… Ah, they've started switching off the lights… I don't actually have any sense of direction. This is not an overstatement. I often get lost in places familiar to me. I'm unable to picture a place from above, only by landmarks. This is why I've got lost so many times in here. Even though I built it. I'm possibly not the best guide.

THIS IS AN ANNOUNCEMENT:

THE FAIR WILL BE CLOSING IN TEN MINUTES.

CHOOSE MY EXIT.

NORTH (p. 205)

SOUTH (p. 206)

EAST (p. 207)

WEST (p. 208)

NORTH

I will continue to focus on translation and writing. I will not waver. I will not doubt the task at hand. I will keep pushing for fair pay. I will form a translators' collective and we will work together to strengthen our power. I will make transparent the conditions I'm working under. Or I will do another job and accept only the projects I really want to translate, and seek out authors who don't often make it out of the German-speaking world. Float towards land in a rubber ring.

SOUTH

I will abandon German and withhold my labour. I will move to Malta for a time. I will learn Maltese and learn the full history of Malta. I will find a job doing anything. I will engage with my heritage in a way that I'm afraid to do. I will put even more energy into publishing Maltese writers, and into Maltese. Sail away in a fishing boat.

EAST

I will stop translating and writing and become a maker, build models, draw, make art, move away from screens and paper and words and use my body. Zoom off on a jet ski.

WEST

I will focus more on my family, my friends, my health, where I live right now. I will continue to teach locally, become supportive of local projects. Instead of writing books, I will do something tangibly useful for the future of the world. And I will train to become an audio-describer and translate another way. Dive into the water.

• • •

Once the ferries have landed,

once everyone has crossed the bridge,

the Fair self-destructs

like a word if you look at it for too long.

A week later, a bottle washes up on Hastings beach. Inside it is a tightly wound scroll of paper. Written on the scroll is:

A manifesto for *fair translation*

I will make a fair go of learning the language I'm trying to translate
I will make a fair go of learning about the culture/s of this language:
its literature, its art forms, its traditions, its history, its food,
its current events
I will give writing creatively, and reading and writing in the forms
I translate, a fair go
I will ask permission from the rights holder of the original; it must
be used fairly
I will make sure quotes in the original are used legally in the translation:
fair use
I will treat my author fairly
I will say when I and others are not treated fairly, and challenge
unfair behaviour
I will be fair with myself
I will rest when I am fairly tired
I will aim for fair health
I will help make sure not every translator is homogenously fair
I will help make sure the way translators are chosen for jobs is as fair
as possible
I will not uphold that every translation must be fair and beautiful,
but simply befitting
I will acknowledge if I have made a mistake, fair cop
I will believe that it is only fair for me to challenge unnuanced criticism
of my work
I will be a fair mediator
I will remember I am a worker within an industry that takes my goods
to fayre
I will ask for my fair share
I will fight for a fair income
I will remember that all/not all projects are fair game to me

I will expect my translations to bear my fair name
I will not expect my translations to be completely fair, blemish-free,
   too clean to read, by a fair hand
I will make a fair piece of work
I will hope for the reader to treat me fairly and without bias

I think 'fair' is a better judge for a translation in a manifest range of meanings: fair as in a *reasonable* try. I have given translating translation a fair go, the way I understand it, the only way I could that didn't seem impossible at the time.

FIN.

Guided Tours

Acknowledgements/Credits

There are a lot of people I would like to thank for helping me write this book.

Thank you to the University of East Anglia for awarding me a fully-funded Studentship (2019–23) to undertake a PhD in Creative and Critical Writing, for which an earlier version of *Fair* was submitted alongside a thesis on hybrid life-writing by literary translators.

Thank you to my supervision team Cecilia Rossi, Tiffany Atkinson and Petra Rau for many years of supporting my research and for their enthusiasm for *Fair* in particular, and for always pushing it to be even more fun. Thank you also to Delphine Grass for supporting and publishing my research.

Thank you to Cove Park for awarding me a Literature and Translation Residency, where I had many epiphanies about this book, and to the judges of the Ivan Juritz Prize 2020 for longlisting an excerpt of *Fair* in the Experimentation in Text category, which was a very welcome boost early on in the project. Thank you to the British Library, the Arts and Humanities Research Council, and the Institute for Modern Languages Research for awarding me the inaugural Translator in Residence position at the British Library (2017–19), where I conducted research for this book.

Thank you to *Wasafiri*, *Inque*, *Bricks from the Kiln*, *the Brixton Review of Books*, *Post45*, the British Centre for Literary Translation, Rough Trade Books, if a leaf falls press and Guadalupe Nettel for publishing excerpts from *Fair* over the years.

Thank you to Kat Storace, Elliot Martin, Richard Phoenix and Rebecca DeWald for your brilliant feedback on earlier drafts.

Thank you to Sophie Collins, Theodora Danek, Kat Storace, Sophie Seita, Polly Barton, Michelle Steinbeck and Gregor Hens for such generous collaborations.

Thank you to Charlotte Ryland, Theodora Danek, Sarah Frappier, Daniel Hahn, Jacques Testard, Karl Smith, Michael Caines, Philip Oltermann and Jennifer Croft for taking a chance on me, believing in my abilities and/or recommending me to others.

Thank you to all the translators I've read and talked with over the years who've helped me develop my thinking about translation and who've kept me going, including: Deborah Smith, Emma Ramadan, Khairani Barokka, Anton Hur, Annie McDermott and Marta Dziurosz. Special shout out to Frank Wynne for saving a translation I lost when my laptop failed and for making me a Wikipedia page.

Thank you to Kate Briggs, who has inspired so many translators to reveal their thinking and feeling.

Thank you to Joe Hales for all the work on *Verfreundungseffekt* and *Fair*, this feels very full circle!

Thank you to Jess Chandler at Prototype for publishing *Fair* – our fourth book together! Your patience, care, positivity and energy are the reasons – literally and motivationally – that I've kept writing.

Thank you to Richard, for everything.

I wish I could mention every single literary translator I know (those I like in any case), but unlike the Fair, the space in the book is finite. Just thinking about literary translators overwhelms me with emotion, and I wrote this book for all of us.

Barton, Polly, *Fifty Sounds* (London: Fitzcarraldo Editions, 2021)

Bellos, David, *Is That a Fish in Your Ear?* (London: Particular Books, 2011)

Bhanot, Kavita and Jeremy Tiang, eds, *Violent Phenomena: 21 Essays on Translation* (London: Tilted Axis Press, 2022)

Briggs, Kate, *This Little Art* (London: Fitzcarraldo Editions, 2017)

Choi, Don Mee, *Translation is a Mode = Translation is an Anti-Neocolonial Mode* (New York: Ugly Duckling Presse, 2020)

Collins, Sophie, ed., *Currently & Emotion: Translations* (London: Test Centre, 2016)

Croft, Jennifer, *Homesick* (Edinburgh: Charco Press, 2022)

Freely, Maureen, *Angry in Piraeus* (London: Sylph Editions, 2014)

Gansel, Mireille, *Translation as Transhumance*, trans. Ros Schwartz (London: Les Fugitives, 2017)

Grossman, Edith, *Why Translation Matters* (London: Yale University Press, 2010)

Hahn, Daniel, *Catching Fire: A Translation Diary* (Edinburgh: Charco Press, 2023)

Karashima, David, *Who We're Reading When We're Reading Murakami* (New York: Soft Skull Press, 2020)

Matthieussent, Brice, *Revenge of the Translator*, trans. Emma Ramadan (Dallas, TX: Deep Vellum Publishing, 2018)

Muir, Willa, *Belonging* (Glasgow: Kennedy & Boyd, 2008)

Nakayasu, Sawako, *Say Translation is Art* (New York: Ugly Duckling Presse, 2020)

Ní Ghríofa, Doireann, *A Ghost in the Throat* (Dublin: Tramp Press, 2020)

Polizzotti, Mark, *Sympathy for the Traitor: A Translation Manifesto* (Cambridge, MA: The MIT Press, 2019)

Rabassa, Gregory, *If This Be Treason: Translation and its Discontents: A Memoir* (New York: New Directions, 2005)

Searls, Damion, *The Philosophy of Translation* (London: Yale University Press, 2025)

Wright, Chantal, *Yoko Tawada's Portrait of a Tongue: An Experimental Translation* (Ottawa: University of Ottawa Press, 2013)

My Translations (selected)

Favorita by Michelle Steinbeck (Faber & Faber, 2026)

Minihorror by Barbi Marković (Faber & Faber, 2025)

The City and the World by Gregor Hens (Fitzcarraldo Editions, 2025)

Milk Teeth by Helene Bukowski (Unnamed Press, 2021 / MTO Press, 2023)

Kleenex/LiLiPUT by Marlene Marder et al (Thrilling Living, 2023)

The Liquid Land by Raphaela Edelbauer (Scribe, 2021)

The Pine Islands by Marion Poschmann (Serpent's Tail, 2019 / Coach House Books, 2020)

The Pixels of Paul Cézanne by Wim Wenders (Faber & Faber, 2018)

My Father was a Man on Land and a Whale in the Water by Michelle Steinbeck (Darf Publishing, 2018)

Dance by the Canal by Kerstin Hensel (Peirene Press, 2017)

Nicotine by Gregor Hens (Fitzcarraldo Editions, 2015 / Other Press, 2016)

Jen Calleja is a poet, writer and essayist who has been widely published, including in *The White Review*, *The London Magazine*, and *Best British Short Stories* (Salt). She was awarded an Authors' Foundation Grant from the Society of Authors to work on her debut novel *Vehicle* (Prototype, 2023), an excerpt of which was shortlisted for the Short Fiction / University of Essex Prize. Jen's short story collection *I'm Afraid That's All We've Got Time For* was published by Prototype in 2020, and *Goblinhood: Goblin as a Mode* was published by Rough Trade Books in 2024. An excerpt from *Fair* was Longlisted for the Ivan Juritz Prize for Experimentation in Text.

Jen has been shortlisted for the Man Booker International Prize, the Oxford-Weidenfeld Prize and the Schlegel-Tieck Prize as a literary translator from German into English and was the inaugural Translator in Residence at the British Library. She is co-founding editor of Praspar Press and played and toured in the DIY punk band Sauna Youth.

( )   (   )   p   prototype

poetry / prose / interdisciplinary projects / anthologies

Creating new possibilities in the publishing
of fiction and poetry through a flexible,
interdisciplinary approach and the production
of unique and beautiful books.

Prototype is an independent publisher working
across genres and disciplines, committed to
discovering and sharing work that exists outside
the mainstream.

Each publication is unique in its form and
presentation, and the aesthetic of each object
is considered critical to its production.

Prototype strives to increase audiences for
experimental writing, as the home for writers
and artists whose work requires a creative vision
not offered by mainstream literary publishers.

In its current, evolving form, Prototype consists
of 4 strands of publications:
> (type 1 — poetry)
> (type 2 — prose)
> (type 3 — interdisciplinary projects)
> (type 4 — anthologies) including an annual
> anthology of new work, *PROTOTYPE*.

Fair: The Life-Art of Translation by Jen Calleja
Published by Prototype in 2025

The right of Jen Calleja to be identified as author of this
work has been asserted in accordance with Section 77
of the UK Copyright, Designs and Patents Act 1988.

Design by Joe Hales studio
Typeset in Enigma (Jeremy Tankard)
Printed in the UK by Bell & Bain Ltd.

ISBNS
978-1-913513-73-3 (standard edition)
978-1-913513-79-5 (special edition)
978-1-913513-74-0 (e-book)

( )   (   )   p   prototype

(type 2 – prose)
www.prototypepublishing.co.uk
@prototypepubs

prototype publishing
71 oriel road
london e9 5sg
uk